CHAPMAN'S ODYSSEY

BY THE SAME AUTHOR

At The Jerusalem

Trespasses

A Distant Likeness

Peter Smart's Confessions

Old Soldiers

An English Madam: The Life and Work of Cynthia Payne

Gabriel's Lament

An Immaculate Mistake: Scenes from Childhood and Beyond

Sugar Cane

Kitty and Virgil

*Three Queer Lives: An Alternative Biography of Naomi Jacob,
Fred Barnes and Arthur Marshall*

Uncle Rudolf

A Dog's Life

CHAPMAN'S ODYSSEY

A Novel

PAUL BAILEY

BLOOMSBURY

NEW YORK · BERLIN · LONDON · SYDNEY

Excerpt from "Acquainted with the Night" from *The Poetry of Robert Frost* edited by Edward Connery Lathem. Copyright © 1928, 1969 by Henry Holt and Company, copyright © 1956 by Robert Frost. Reprinted by permission of Henry Holt and Company, LLC.

Every reasonable effort has been made to trace the copyright holders of material reproduced in this book, but if any have been inadvertently overlooked the publishers would be glad to hear from them.

Published by Bloomsbury USA, New York

All papers used by Bloomsbury USA are natural, recyclable products made from wood grown in well-managed forests. The manufacturing processes conform to the environmental regulations of the country of origin.

LIBRARY OF CONGRESS CATALOGING-IN-PUBLICATION DATA

Bailey, Paul, 1937–
Chapman's odyssey / by Paul Bailey. — 1st U.S. ed.
p. cm.
ISBN 978-1-60819-821-4
1. Hospital patients—Fiction. 2. Psychological fiction.
I. Title.
PR6052.A319C33 2012
823'.914—dc23
2011029642

First U.S. Edition 2012

10 9 8 7 6 5 4 3 2 1

Typeset by Hewer Text UK Ltd, Edinburgh
Printed in the U.S.A. by Quad/Graphics, Fairfield, Pennsylvania

In fond memory of

Sandra Davis Sinclair

1933–2006

I wish to express my deep and abiding gratitude to the trustees of the Royal Literary Fund for the generous support they have given me in recent years.

Saturday Evening

SO HERE HE was at last, where he had long feared to be.

He heard a gentle voice assuring Mr Chapman that he was in the safest of safe hands, that he would be receiving the best care in the world.

— My name is Nancy Driver, that same voice informed him. — Sister Nancy Driver. I and my nursing team will be looking after you.

— Yes?

— Yes, yes. Day and night. Night and day.

Should he offer thanks in advance? Should he even say anything?

— No need to speak. Leave everything to us.

— Yes?

— Yes, Mr Chapman.

— I am very tired, he said after a silence, angrily.

— Of course you are. Don't tire yourself further. You need rest.

— I suppose I do.

Suppose? 'Suppose' was one of Harry Chapman's most-used words, to the irritation at times of his friends and relatives. He liked to suppose where others stated, secure in their certainties. He favoured suppositions, those delicate stepping stones towards truth. He supposed, now, that he needed the rest Sister Driver was proposing. Was there, in fact, an alternative to consider?

— You're smiling, Mr Chapman. That's good.

— Is it? Why?

— You are very inquisitive, Mr Chapman.

— I am. I always have been.

He wanted to add 'I always will be', but a sudden sense of the inappropriateness of such a remark prevented him.

— I'm a questioning spirit, Sister Driver. That's what I'm noted for.

— Smiling is good because it shows you have a positive attitude.

When was it, in his lifetime, that people first spoke of attitudes that are either positive or negative? In his childhood, they were happy or sad, those people, depending on their characters. No one, then, described a miserable neighbour as having a negative attitude, and his limitlessly cheerful Aunt Rose, who looked on the bright side when there was no brightness visible, would have been mystified to hear that her attitude to the problems she refused to acknowledge with more than a few slightly clouded moments of reflection was of the positive kind.

— I am of a melancholy disposition, Sister Driver. My smiles aren't what they seem.

— Is that the case? Are you a mischief maker, Mr Chapman?

— Possibly.

— My daddy was the same, bless his soul. My poor mother never knew quite where she was with him. He liked to talk in riddles.

— You'll find that I make myself clear, Sister Driver. Or may I address you as Nancy?

— Of course you may.

— It's such a resonant name to my old ears.

— My parents were fond of the song 'Nancy with the Laughing Face'. That's how I came by it.

— Really? I can't recall why Frank and Alice saddled me with Harry. But Harry I am, and Harry is what I want you to call me.

— I shall. Thank you, Harry. I'll leave you to rest. Try and sleep.

He'd wanted to continue with the banal conversation, to hear more about Nancy's mischievous daddy and bewildered mother. There are times, and this was one of them, when even a man as sophisticated as Harry Chapman requires nothing more from life than trivial chit-chat, the constant trickle of the insignificant. He could tell already that Sister Nancy was a skilled practitioner in the art of saying the sweet and comforting words of little consequence and he was grateful, he supposed, for her artistry. Yes, gratitude, for the moment, was in order.

He dozed, and very soon the ward, with its monitors and forbidding instruments of healing, evaporated. He was no longer in bed, but walking – slowly, of necessity – through dense fog. It was a pea-souper, a London particular, and he was making his wary way homewards. He covered his nose and mouth with the handkerchief his mother had ironed that November morning, but it offered only meagre protection against the foul and poisonous air that was soon filling his lungs. The faint light of a street lamp on the corner near the gasworks gave him his bearings – he had only to turn left, then right, and he would be warm and comfortable again, breathing easily as he sat on his special chair at the kitchen table, ready and eager for his evening meal. What would it be tonight? A stew, he hoped, with chunks of meat and diced winter vegetables and pearl barley. There might be dumplings, too.

He quickened his step, spurred on by the grumbling noises in his belly. The familiar road seemed to have gained more houses, barely discernible though they were, and the usually modest front gardens, drab at the year's end, now boasted exotic shrubs. Where, oh where, was number 96? He had recently read the fairy tales collected by the Brothers Grimm and he was given to wonder if some malevolent giant or witch had spirited number 96 away, complete with his mother and sister Jessie as well as the family who occupied the rooms on the ground floor. He smiled at the fanciful notion, even as he realised that numbers 94 and 98 stood next to each other, with nothing in between. His home and family had gone, taking his supper with them. He felt like weeping for the stew he was destined never to eat.

— Harry?

Whose voice was this? It was too soft and low to be his mother's or sister's, or indeed any of his women friends.

— Harry, it's Nancy.

— Who?

A moment passed before he recognised Sister Driver, who was stroking his hand and smiling. He was back in the ward. There were screens around his bed, and a cherubic-looking man with dark curly hair was standing beside her, holding a clipboard.

— Harry, meet Dr Pereira.

— Pereira?

— My father is Spanish.

— But you have a Scots accent.

— That's because my mother's Scottish. She brought me up. Mr Chapman, I'm not here to talk about myself.

— Come closer, Dr Pereira. I want to get a good look at you.

The doctor stepped forward, and the patient stared at him intently before asking:

— Who is it you remind me of?

— I've no idea. Who is it I remind you of?

— Let me think.

— Please do, Mr Chapman.

— It's a painting.

— A flattering one, I trust?

— Definitely.

— There you are, Dr Pereira, said Sister Driver.

— A fresco. That's it. A fresco.

Yes, yes, a fresco, in Italy, first sighted during that marvellous late summer and early autumn of 1968, when he walked contentedly in Mediterranean sunlight, even while the sky was overcast.

— Your double is in the Brancacci Chapel in the church of Santa Maria del Carmine. He's on the far right of the fresco called *The Dispute with Simon Magus* and he's staring straight out at the viewer with his large brown eyes. He is the painter himself, Filippino Lippi, according to the experts.

— Where is this church?

— In Florence.

— Perhaps I shall see it one day.

— You could be Lippi's reincarnation.

— Let's talk about you now, Mr Chapman, if you please.

He listened as best he could to what Dr Pereira was telling him. An enema might be necessary, an endoscopy would certainly highlight the problem, but there were other possibilities.

— I am going to give you an injection. It will relax you and make you feel drowsy.

Sister Driver located a vein in his right arm, swabbed it, and then the doctor inserted the needle, assuring Mr

Chapman that he would pass a relatively comfortable night.

How relative was relatively, and how comfortable comfortable? he was tempted to ask. He had spoken too much already and had exhausted himself remembering the face of Filippino Lippi for the benefit, if such it was, of Dr Pereira. He would save his breath.

The good Sister Nancy plumped up his pillows and told him Dr Pereira, who had now left, was the pride of the hospital, despite his being so young. He had a bright future, if anyone had. He was certain to climb to the top of the medical tree.

— You mark my words, Harry.

Oh, he'd mark her words if it were possible, if he lived well into the doctor's bright future, which he very much doubted he would. He was seventy, for Christ's sake, and Filippino Lippi's lookalike was in his twenties, it seemed. He remembered, then, that Alice had died in her ninetieth year and that the lifeline on the palm of his right hand promised longevity. Was that a promise Nature intended to keep?

— I hope not, he surprised himself by muttering.

— Do you want something, Harry?

— No.

What he wanted was to be out of this place, out of this bed, out in the world once more, himself entire. Those were his four wants at this precise moment, and obviously not to be granted.

— Want on, as his mother was fond of saying. Just you want on, Harry.

Was it courtesy of Dr Pereira's wonder drug that he was hearing her now, her naturally harsh voice sharpened by hurt and disappointment? No night could be comfortable

6

in her presence, not even relatively, and if Dr Pereira, he of the curly hair and steady brown gaze, were here her son would tell him so.

— That was always your trouble, wanting what you couldn't have.

— Rest, rest, perturbèd spirit, he said, relishing her confusion.

He savoured the silence that followed. The injection appeared to be taking effect, for his whole body was suddenly weightless. He was floating on the surface of a calm sea.

Or so he imagined, until another voice, as faint as it was hoarse, spoke his name.

— Who are you?

He was curious to identify the stranger.

— You don't recognise me?

— I can scarcely hear you.

— I have not much to say. I have no reason to speak louder.

He thought he detected a subtle American twang, suggestive of a refined New England upbringing, perhaps.

— Then why are you bothering to talk to me?

— I am bothering to talk to you because I cannot – no, I must not – be bothered.

— Did I meet you in New York?

— You have met me in many places. We have been companions of a kind in London and in Rome and once, I do believe, in Calcutta. I am unusually verbose tonight. I am, usually, a man of very few, necessary words. That is my customary condition.

And this is madness, Harry Chapman thought, to be communing with someone who never lived, except in the pages of a little book.

— Are you still there?

He was relieved that there was no answer. Of course Bartleby wasn't there. It had been the purest lunacy to have imagined that he ever was.

The drowsiness Dr Pereira had predicted now overcame him. Sleep, welcome sleep, was bearing him gently away.

— Thank you, Doctor.

— My pleasure.

For an hour and more it was as if he was no one. He slept as a newborn baby is said to sleep, in that blessed time before memory, before the dawning of consciousness. His heartbeat was regular, his breathing normal. The equipment at his bedside registered tranquillity to the nurse on duty.

He awoke at five thirty in the morning, wondering where he was.

Sunday

THERE WAS A church not far from the hospital, its
bells summoning the faithful to celebration and prayer.
He loved churches, always had, even after he'd shaken off
the notion of a God who actually cared about the sorrows
and trials of humankind. He recalled, now, his childhood
visits to St Mary's, nestling in a bend of the Thames. He
had been baptised there, 'born of water and the spirit', on
a cold March Sunday, and it was there, during his school's
Christmas service of thanksgiving, thirteen years onwards,
that he stepped into the pulpit and recited from memory
some lines of Milton – the fourth and fifth stanzas of his
Hymn on the Morning of Christ's Nativity.

> *No War, or battles sound*
> *Was heard the World around,*
> *The idle spear and shield were high up hung;*
> *The hookèd chariot stood*
> *Unstain'd with hostile blood,*
> *The Trumpet spake not to the armèd throng . . .*

— What was that you were mumbling, Mr Chapman?
It sounded very old-fashioned, the little I could make
of it.

— It's a poem, Nurse. It's been in my head for more than fifty years along with a hundred others.

— Are you a professor?

— I was called the Professor when I was young. It was a family joke. My nose was forever in a book, my mother said.

— I wish my son read books.

— What does he do instead?

— Plays games on his computer.

— When is Sister Driver back on duty?

— You miss her, do you? Is there a romance blooming?

— Yes to the first question, no to the second.

— She's on tonight, you naughty man.

Oh, the coquetry of the nursing profession. He corrected himself: the coquetry of *some* members of the nursing profession. At least Nurse Mullen wasn't calling him 'sweetheart' and 'darling', the terms of endearment that signalled certain death.

He waited for the first 'sweetheart', the first 'darling', from Nurse Mullen's noticeably thin lips. They were not, as yet, forthcoming.

— It isn't every patient who spouts poetry to himself.

'To spout': the verb was one of his mother's favourites. Whenever she saw him act, she accused him of spouting. He pictured a jet of words, like the foam a whale emits, gushing from his mouth.

— Why did you say that?

— Say what, Mr Chapman?

— 'Spouts poetry'. Why 'spouts'?

— Well, it stands to reason, if you think about it.

— Please explain.

— Well, poetry isn't a normal way of speaking, is it? I'm not talking in verses, am I? That's the reason poetry's always spouted when it's read out loud.

— Ah, yes. Thank you.

— You've got a wicked smile on your face.

— It's not on my arse, Nurse Mullen.

— I'm going to love you and leave you. Doctor will be coming round shortly.

He returned her ridiculous, coquettish wave. He felt like blowing her a ridiculous, coquettish kiss but refrained from doing so. The pain in his gut had returned, barring all attempts at levity.

— Christ Almighty, he whispered.

No earthly use invoking the son of God, he thought. He and his ancient pa won't waste their celestial time on an old reprobate like you.

— Good morning, Mr Chapman. And how are we feeling today?

— We? I'm not royal, I do assure you. I am a common or garden queen and a lifelong republican.

— I am here to offer you spiritual comfort, if you require it.

— How very kind, Reverend. I am sorry to disappoint you but I have my own spiritual resources. I shall be my own comforter. You're Roman Catholic, I assume. You made the sign of the cross when I exposed myself as an ordinary queen.

— Yes. I am Father Terence.

— Allow me to ask you a theological question, if I may.

— Please do.

— When I was five years old I nearly died of diphtheria. It was one of the diseases that afflicted poor families. My mother became a regular churchgoer – Anglican, Father – throughout the eighteen months I waited for death's door to open. If it had opened, as it almost did, where would I have gone to all those years ago?

— Were you a good little boy?

— I had no desire to be bad.

— Then I think a home would have been found for you in heaven.

— Not limbo?

— No, Mr Chapman. I am not alone in regarding limbo as a literary concept. You had been baptised, yes?

— Yes.

— Heaven, without a doubt.

— Oh, Father Terence, what a happy little soul I might have been, playing with my other infant friends for all eternity. Are toys allowed up there?

— Toys lead to squabbles and envy. No toys. Just you as you were born, naked and unadorned and blessed by the Holy Spirit.

— And look at me now, as unblessed as you can get. I am wasting your time. There must be people in here in serious need of your attentions. Thank you for talking to me.

— God bless you.

That was the longest conversation he'd had with a priest in years, he realised when the amiable Father Terence departed. He'd had no cause to converse with clerics, to put it pompously. He had spoken nothing less than the beautiful truth when he'd told the father he had his own spiritual resources. Step forward sweet-tempered George Herbert, heartless but transcendental John Donne, radiant and disconsolate Christopher Smart, virginal sexpot Teresa of Ávila, stoical Marcus Aurelius. His chorus line of comforters was unending.

— He seemed a nice man for a Catholic, he heard his mother say. — Why everyone can't be Church of England is something I've never understood. I'm glad you were polite to him. You can be so rude to clergymen when you want to.

— Mea culpa.

— What are you talking about? You do it to annoy me, speaking foreign. And why did you have to tell that Holy Father you nearly died of diphtheria? You have a morbid streak, Harry. You always did have.

— Always?

— As far back as I can remember. I swear you came out of my womb in a temper. You didn't look pleased to be here.

— I wanted his expert opinion. He gave it to me. He said I would have gone to heaven if, if –

— There was no 'if', was there?

— If, if I wasn't here now, listening to you again. If I'd been 'gathered', as you were fond of saying. If, if, if, Mother mine.

— Get back in your pram, Harry Chapman.

That taunt for all his childhood; that lethal combination of five short words intended to diminish him; oh, the terrible inference that he would never grow into the kind of manhood she might approve of – here it was, harshly expressed, unsettling him, angering him, in this hospital ward, in a changed London, on the eve of his seventieth birthday.

— I'm seventy, Mum.

— Seventy? Seven, seventeen or seventy, you're still the same useless object I brought into the world.

— It's good to have your support.

He reminded himself that Alice Chapman had been dead for twenty-two years. To his and Jessie's amazement, she had left instructions that she wished to be cremated. The urn containing her ashes had been buried in St Peter's churchyard in the small country town where she had been born and raised. Yet here she was, in some form or another, goading him with the familiar words of long ago.

— Mr Chapman? Mr Chapman?

He came out of his gruesome reverie and saw Dr Pereira.

— Nurse Mullen tells me you were sick this morning.

— I was.

— Immediately after breakfast. Is that correct?

— Yes.

— You will be given no more solid food for the time being. You will be fed intravenously.

— I understand.

— Until we discover exactly what is wrong with you.

— Why the delay?

— We have to be absolutely certain, Mr Chapman.

A saline drip was duly attached to him later that morning and a card with the instruction NIL BY MOUTH placed above his head.

— I feel trapped.

— Don't talk silly, said a nurse called Marybeth Myslawchuk, as her name tag informed him. — This is for your benefit. You're not trapped one teensy bit.

— You sound American.

— I sound Canadian, if that's all right by you. I sound Canadian because that's what I am.

— I do apologise.

— No need to. Since you are so curious, my family hails originally from Ukraine.

— I was in Lvov once. A pretty place, with some interesting Italianate architecture.

— Never been there, and I can't say I want to go. My grandpa and grandma were happy to get out, and I am more than happy to be in jolly old England, where it's never too hot or too cold. That's me in a nutshell, Mr Harry Chapman.

— No one can be contained in a nutshell, Marybeth Myslawchuk. Oh, I do hope I pronounced that second name even half correctly.

— Nine out of ten for trying, Mr C. More emphasis on the 'mys' and you'd be perfect. The word's going round the ward that you know a whole lot of poetry.

— I do.

— Say some for me, then. That's a polite request.

It was the easiest poem to remember. It was in his bloodstream, had been there since he was a skinny boy of twelve, when love – with its delights and sadnesses – was still on the horizon, but the beauty of his inherited language had already established itself in his mind and heart, the two indistinguishable. So he serenaded the plump, middle-aged Canadian by enquiring if he should compare her to a summer's day, and assuring her in thirteen more lines of his undying affection, surviving beyond the grave.

They were both silent when he had finished. He was slightly embarrassed, as if the feelings he had expressed were his very own and their object the stately Nurse Marybeth. It was almost as if he had been wooing her.

— Well, Mr Chapman, you're a Shakespearean son of a gun, if I ever heard one. That was a treat. I thank you.

He thanked her for thanking him, so touched was he by her response.

— That's enough thank-yous for today, thank you very much. And no more silly talk of being trapped.

Silly talk or not, he did feel trapped now, waiting here for his friend Graham to arrive from Sri Lanka, where he had gone to take stock of his life so far and to contemplate his future. Graham was in the jungle somewhere, dressed only in a sarong, in a hut by the side of a lake, cut off from all contact with the West. No electricity, no telephone, nothing. Oh, the luxury, Harry Chapman thought, of going native for the purpose of self-improvement, thousands of miles from civilisation and its discontents.

Almost the last person he had seen before the unbearable pain had sent him phoning for an ambulance was the woman known to the cognoscenti as the Duchess of Bombay. She was standing outside his house in her customary makeshift clothing – a tattered Napoleonic overcoat, a faded cotton dress, brown stockings rolled down below her knees and those improvised shoes composed of scraps of newspaper and plastic bags – and shouting abuse at the world. Her adversary had to be the entire universe for there was nobody else in view. The Duchess, in her remote youth, had trained to be a concert pianist. As Anya Lipschitz (born Anne Lipton) she had played Grieg's Piano Concerto with an orchestra made up of former students of London's music colleges, and had given two well-received solo recitals, the last at Wigmore Hall in 1959. On that memorable evening, she performed an eclectic repertoire: a Chopin polonaise; a fantasia by Liszt; some early pieces of Alban Berg; five of Brahms's intermezzi and Beethoven's 'Les Adieux' sonata. There were several encores.

That was the beginning, and the end, of her fame. Two things destroyed her potentially brilliant career – the sudden death of her parents in an air crash in France, and the arrival of a young man from Istanbul with whom she became captivated and then infatuated. She was now very rich, thanks to her father's bequest, and for the next three years she lived solely for Acil, in a large house in west London she leased. It was her love nest in that quiet, tree-lined street whenever Acil was there with her, and her desolate moated grange when he was inexplicably absent. Each time he returned she attempted to be calm and reasonable, trying and failing to conquer the jealousy that possessed her. To console him, because he was always the injured party, she bought him tailored suits, handmade shirts and shoes, expensive – and, to her eyes, rather vulgar – items of jewellery. He liked to remind her that she was lucky to have such a handsome and virile lover, and then she thanked him for bestowing upon her the favours most women could only dream of – yes, yes, she assured him, she knew just how lucky she was.

All this she had recounted to Harry Chapman, in snatches of conversation over two decades, on fine or clouded afternoons, in the course of chance encounters. Her need to reveal her past to him depended entirely on the mood she was in, for sometimes she was vindictive and laconic, her eyes blazing with anger, her mouth pursed contemptuously. Her narrative, given the deranged state of her mind, was surprisingly continuous: it was not until she had dealt with Acil's final departure that she ventured to talk of her afterlife, as she referred to it. He heard of her descent into depression, her eviction from the house, her bankruptcy, and her overpowering reliance on the temporary comfort afforded by Bombay Sapphire, her favoured gin. For a terrible while, she was the leading lady in a troupe of public guzzlers who gathered together, existence permitting, on a forlorn strip of grass, intended as a communal garden, near a busy roundabout. One of their number, a perpetually defeated Irishman called Colum, had honoured her with the title of Duchess of Bombay – in respect of her refined way of speaking, her briefly flickering intelligence and her obvious hauteur (a word, she explained to a bemused Harry Chapman, decidedly not in Colum's vocabulary). She was the brightest star in a belching, hiccuping, incoherent firmament, and she played her appointed role with, she told him, a regrettable relish. She was a somebody – she'd had a wonder-filled past as Anya Lipschitz – among an assortment of nobodies. The troupe disbanded, courtesy of the Grim Reaper, who took Sean and Seamus and Muriel and Betsy and Eamon and who-knows-whom-else in his icy clasp. She found herself an isolated survivor who no longer craved company. She had arrived at a state of almost complete solitariness. Almost, yes, but not quite, because she still cared to convey her sorrows to a man she did not know as Harry Chapman. He was her appreciative port in a seemingly lasting storm. He listened to her every word.

He was in the library one morning when he saw her chosen name on the spine of a very slim book. It was a study of the life and music of Anton von Webern, and he could tell immediately that it was written with graceful lucidity. Could it be possible there was another Anya Lipschitz, an authority on the twelve-tone technique Webern had pioneered? This Anya was fluent in German, to judge by her translations of the composer's writings, as well as being a skilled explicator of his intricate works. No, he decided, this was a different Anya, a scholar unlikely to be deceived and abased by a Turkish gigolo. She was, surely, too wise to have surrendered herself to such an obviously professional charmer.

Was she, or was she not, the scholarly Anya? The question remained unanswered for several months, because the Duchess of Bombay and the battered car in which she had made her home had vanished from the district. The vehicle, he learned, had been pronounced a threat to health, the Duchess's cavalier way with discarded food greatly attracting the local rodent population, thus causing it to be removed on the instructions of the borough council. It was scrap by the time he went to visit her. Then he assumed she was dead, gone where her inebriated courtiers had gone, and he was too occupied with the novel he was struggling to write to bother about identifying the author of *Anton von Webern: A Life in Music*. The Duchess was relegated to the back of his mind.

On a chilly November day he heard her call out to him.

— You. You. Come over here, you.

She was sitting on a doorstep, rubbing butter onto her legs.

— Taking precautions for the winter. Nothing like butter to keep the cold out.

— How are you? Where have you been?

— You can see how I am. I've been nowhere.

He asked her if she knew anything about the Austrian composer Webern. She replied by humming a fragment of his youthful passacaglia.

— Did you write a book about him?

— Perhaps I did, and perhaps I didn't.

That was answer enough. He decided not to pursue the subject. Besides, he had no alternative, for now she dismissed him with a curt 'Go away'.

— Goodbye, he said, and left.

And then there she was, on Saturday, yards from his house, howling like Lear on the heath although it was a balmy September afternoon, the light gently autumnal. As he watched her from a first-floor window, the pain in his stomach assumed an agonising new dimension. He picked up the phone and dialled 999 and asked for A & E. He waited, crouched on the carpet, for the ambulance to arrive. When it did, he could only mumble that he had been constipated for a week and he didn't know why. He was usually regular. The paramedics, a young man and younger woman, advised him not to speak any more, to take it easy, to try not to worry. They would be at the hospital in double-quick time. The local football team was playing away in the north of England and the roads, for once, were free of excess traffic.

— Harry?

— Is that you, Sister Nancy?

— None other.

— Is it night already?

— No, no. I came in early. I have masses of paperwork to get through.

— I envy you.

— What on earth do you mean?

— My work's paperwork, Nancy. I should like to be at my desk, mulling over the next sentence. That's why I'm envious. My hands are useless in here.

— Try not to fret too much.

Nancy Driver's voice, he thought with a smile, is ever soft, gentle and low, an excellent thing in woman.

— I'll try.

— That's my Harry. What's that old saying? 'Smile and the world smiles with you, weep and you weep alone.' Is that how it goes?

— I'm afraid so.

— You have that mischievous twinkle in your eye.

— My eye's the best place for it.

The nurse named Marybeth had joined Sister Nancy at his bedside.

— Has he recited a poem for you, Sister?

— You've lost me, Marybeth.

— Mr Chapman is a living and breathing anthology. He serenaded me with a Shakespeare sonnet this morning. He was word-perfect.

— Well, well. We've never had a patient who entertained us with poetry. The odd singer, yes. There was that fat Welshman who burst into song if you so much as glanced at him.

— Oh my God, what a caterwauler he was. I'd have cheerfully strangled him, had I been given the opportunity.

— I nearly had, and I nearly did, said Sister Nancy. The two women laughed at the revelation of their shared guilty secret. Or so Harry Chapman supposed.

— Now then, Mr Chapman, Sister Driver is waiting to hear your dulcet tones.

— Is she?

— I am, Harry. If you would be so kind. Something short and sweet.

He asked them to wait. He had to think. He needed to conjure up a poem that suited the sister's requirements. There was a host he could choose from.

— This should do the trick.

How old was he when he committed the little beauty to memory? His teacher, Mr Robertson, had copied it out for him from a yellowing book in his collection. Yes, he was thirteen, and precociously addicted to Elizabethan poetry, and Mr Robertson, knowing his taste, had picked out this gem for him. He had learned it on a late afternoon in early spring, making it his own as he strolled alongside the Thames at Chelsea.

Would it come back to him now? Was it still there in its brief entirety? He took a breath, and began.

> — *The lowest trees have tops, the ant her gall,*
> *The fly her spleen, the little spark his heat;*
> *Hairs cast their shadows, though they be but small,*
> *And bees have stings, although they be not great.*
> *Seas have their source, and so have shallow springs,*
> *And love is love, in beggars and in kings.*

He paused, looked at his rapt (he hoped) listeners, and continued.

— The ermine hath the fairest skin on earth,
Yet does she choose the Weasel for her peer;
The panther hath a sweet perfumed breath,
Yet doth she suffer apes to draw her near.
No flower more fresh than is the damask rose,
Yet next her side the nettle often grows.

He stopped once more, and signalled to the nurse and the sister that there was one last stanza.

— Where waters smoothest run, deep'st are the fords,
The dial stirs, though none perceive it move;
The fairest faith is in the sweetest words,
The turtles sing not love, and yet they love.
True hearts have eyes and ears, no tongues to speak,
They hear and see, and sigh, and then they break.

— That's it, ladies.
   — It's deep, that's for certain.
   — I liked the beggars and kings.
   — I should explain, he said, enjoying his pedantry — that the hairs that 'cast their shadows' are the hairs on one's body, not the hares you eat jugged.
   — Is that by Shakespeare, too?
   — No, Nurse Myslawchuk.
   — Tell us who wrote it, Harry.
   — I can't. The poet's name is lost in history. It might be his only poem for all I know. He's one of hundreds, perhaps thousands, grouped under the title Anonymous. You could say, if you were fanciful, that his soul lives on whenever someone reads him. That's what I like to believe.

Was he sounding pompous? Impossibly high-minded? What did it matter?

— I can be very serious, Nancy, when the mood hits me.

— You don't need to apologise. It's been lovely listening to you. Hasn't it, Marybeth?

— Surely.

— We'll be your captive audience again tomorrow, Harry.

After they had gone, he felt a momentary glow of satisfaction. He hadn't spoken, or spouted, 'The Lowest Trees Have Tops', in – oh, what – twenty, thirty years? – and yet, minutes past, he had rejoiced in each of its sweet cadences, precisely recalled and thoughtfully delivered.

— Don't get too pleased with yourself. Your head's big enough as it is.

There she was again, the perpetual dampener of every prideful feeling, her bottomless bucket of ice-cold water perpetually at hand.

— Leave me alone, can't you?

— I can't and I won't. You didn't leave me alone when you put me in a book.

— I tried to understand you.

— Is that what you were doing?

— Yes, it was.

— Well, you didn't succeed.

— How would you know? You couldn't read it. You never read my books when you were alive, and this one was written after you were dead.

— Playing safe, were you? Thought I wouldn't notice?

He willed himself to be sensible. It was his own idiotic conscience that was summoning up her rasping tones; that, and his inability, even at this late stage in life, to shake off the mockery she had inflicted on him and Jessie after her husband's sudden death that faraway November. She'd hated Frank for dying once her grief had subsided and her taunts had been fuelled by the anger she felt at being abandoned. He and his sister could only guess at the cause of her malevolence and then learn to endure it until, for him, it became unendurable.

He wasn't hungry – the drip was supplying him with the necessary vitamins – but his thoughts were now of food. It was dinner time in the ward and the smells of curry and cabbage and something his nostrils couldn't identify were reminding him, achingly, of meals he'd prepared or savoured. He recalled, as he lay there helpless, a soup of fennel and fava beans he had consumed on a chilly December night in Palermo. He had ordered a second bowl of it, so entranced was he by its subtle taste, its heavenly aroma. Closing his eyes, he pictured once again its warming, welcoming greenness.

— Come on, Harry, our lives won't be worth living if we're late for Sunday dinner. Your mother's been cooking all morning, getting herself in a terrible sweat, like she does.

They left the park, where his elderly father – his impossibly elderly father – had been playing bowls with his ancient companions. They walked briskly against the wind, with Frank every so often consulting his pocket watch to ensure they would arrive home at the expected time.

— Ten minutes, Harry. Put a step on it. Ten minutes and we're safe. Twelve or fifteen minutes and we're done for.

They'd been done for in the past, with Alice complaining loudly about her husband's lack of consideration.

— You're teaching that son of yours your own bad habits.

— He's your son, too, woman.

— Sit down and eat, the pair of you. Jessie and me have already partaken, as the posh folks say.

They sat and ate the lamb or the beef or the pork or – once or twice a year – the chicken. There were vegetables

24

aplenty: peas and runner beans in summer; turnips and Brussels sprouts and parsnips in winter; potatoes in every season in various guises.

— That was the last meal I had with you and Jessie and your mummy, his father was saying, interrupting his reveries of Alice's plain but satisfying cuisine.

— Was it, Dad?

— Yes, son. I started dying two days later, if you remember. Talking in my not-very-sleepy sleep.

— I came home from school at four in the afternoon. You were lying in the bed Mum shared with Jessie. Your face was covered in sweat. You were shouting at people I'd never heard of.

— They were my comrades in the trenches, Harry. My mates in Flanders. They'd all gone ahead of me. They were ghosts.

— As you are. As you must be.

There was no answer. Silence prevailed. He wanted to eat the unusual soup, a grilled lemon sole, a piece of cheese – Taleggio, perhaps, or Manchego – and drink a chilled Sancerre and then something robust from Sardinia. He longed to share this feast with one of his friends, with all his friends, with Graham, some day soon. He would be cook, however fragile his health, whatever fate the medics decided was in store for him.

— I love that chocolate mousse you make, Harry.

— I know you do, Jessie dear.

— It's that flavour of rosemary I like so much. Do it for me the next time you ask me round to your house.

— How can I say no?

He could say no because she wasn't alive any more. She'd died – when? – three years ago, very suddenly, in that London hospital most resembling a luxury hotel. She had asked him and Graham to let her know what happened in her favourite television soap opera that evening: would the mad Indian solicitor murder her shopkeeper lover, as she threatened to do in the previous instalment?

— We'll record it for you, Jess, said Graham, taking her cold hand and kissing it.

— I haven't missed an episode in twenty-five years.

— There's devotion to duty.

As they were watching the solicitor rolling her lustrous eyeballs, the telephone rang. Graham received the news that Miss Chapman was gravely ill. She needed to see her brother desperately. Their journey back to the hospital tested Graham's driving skills to the limit, for it was raining cats and dogs and elephants and rhinosceroses. The downpour was tropical in its intensity – they might have been in the Philippines, or India during the monsoon season, not southwest London. They arrived too late for a last goodbye.

The crazy Indian solicitor, he told his sister's corpse, was still hatching a plot to trap the shopkeeper. It wasn't quite clear what the vicious bitch had in mind, but if her manic eyes were any indication it was going to be a very nasty trap indeed.

— I'll make the chocolate mousse in your memory, Jess. As soon as I get out of here.

That was a promise he might be able to keep, he hoped.

— Typical, typical, said his inescapable, malevolent mother. — You and your promises, Harry.

— Be quiet, he heard himself shout.

— Is something the matter, Mr Chapman? (It was the nurse called Mullen who was asking the question.) — Who are you bawling at?

— Oh, anyone and no one. The world, I assume. It must be due to the drug Dr Pereira gave me.

— I've come to take some blood from you, if I may.

— Be my bloody guest. I thought you took some yesterday when I first came in.

— We did. But we need some more.

— You ghouls.

The blood left his body. It looked almost black, unlike the bright red gore that seeped from the wounded in films. It was, he thought, the colour of decay.

— Cheer up, Mr Chapman.

Why the hell, why the fuck, should I? he refrained from saying.

— I shall try, Nurse Mullen.

— That's the spirit.

Ah, yes, that's the spirit. He smiled at the nurse, to indicate the spirit was in him and with him. It was the falsest of smiles, but she seemed not to notice its falsity.

— Be brave, she said, and vanished.

What a tiresome creature, what an unwanted pain in the arse, what a nasty piece of moralising work Nurse Mullen was turning out to be.

— You pious cunt, he muttered.

— Wash your mouth out, Harry Chapman, with carbolic soap and water. That is a word I never thought I'd hear on your clever lips. And I don't wish to hear it again. That poor nurse is only doing her duty.

— She didn't catch what I said.

— Whether she did or she didn't isn't the point, Harry Foulmouth Chapman. If I was there, I'd give you a slap across the chops harder than the one I gave you when you came out with that other word.

(Oh, yes. They were walking past the gasworks on a day in June. He was twelve, and innocent. 'What does "fuck" mean, Mum?' he'd asked, and within seconds his whole face was smarting.)

27

— Well, you aren't here, except in my deluded imagination.

But not, he considered, out of her harm's way. It was because he was here – trapped, and dependent upon nurses and doctors – that his restless mind was taken up with old slights, old scores, old barriers to his once longed-for liberty.

— Please cure me, Dr Pereira.

It wasn't his curly-haired saviour who stood before him now. It was someone altogether more haggard, wearing a frock coat, a silk cravat, a discreet waistcoat, finely tapered trousers and boots with a shine that reflected the instruments at his, Harry Chapman's, bedside. Here was a man from another age, yet a recognisable friend.

— Is that you, Pip?

— Yes, Harry.

— You didn't marry her, did you?

— Estella? No. You ask me that same question every time we meet. Mr Dickens didn't want me to, as you know. It was the idea of that sentimental scribbler Bulwer-Lytton. Sentimentalists thrive on happy endings. Estella broke my young heart, Harry. It's still in need of repair. Marry her? No, no, no.

Harry Chapman recalled his first encounter with Philip Pirrip, he of the great expectations, a lifetime ago. Pip's dilemma was to become his own, for he would be ashamed of his uneducated mother, his gauche and awkward sister, his country-bumpkin and cockneyfied London relations. He had discovered refinement in school – poetry; the music of Mozart and Beethoven; the thrilling idea of a life of the mind – and the drabness he came back to each evening in the terraced house in south London caused him to hate the values, if such they were, of his ancestors. How dare they, living in the world, settle for a poverty of spirit that exactly mirrored the poverty they were subjected to by an unjust society? He understood, at fourteen, that you can be rich in intellect, endlessly rich, while poor financially. Then he discovered Pip, the orphaned boy of humble means who is taken from his brother-in-law's forge, where he is to be apprenticed as a blacksmith, and sent off to learn how to be a gentleman and function in polite society. The young Harry was held spellbound by Pip's progress from ungainly Kentish yokel to debonair city butterfly, thanks to the mysterious benefactor whose identity is only revealed when the story moves on to a more exalted plane, with Pip's redemption through suffering, remorse and penitence.

— I haven't gone away, Harry.

— I can't expect you not to stir from my side, dear Pip.

In March 1994, in Calcutta, he'd had the only super-natural experience of his agnostic's life. He had entered the Park Street cemetery in the full blaze of noon and found himself surrounded by the monuments for the illustrious British dead — judges, governors, architects, bridge build-ers, doctors, generals, colonels, majors; an entire galaxy of the once powerful — and saw that people were resting from the heat, or eating their meagre lunches, or sleeping soundly in the coolness of the mausoleums. A wizened, toothless old man who spoke nothing but Bengali handed him a crudely typed guide to the cemetery in even cruder English and kept his palm open until the visitor had filled it with small coins. The man clutched his sleeve and led him to the grave he had come to see — the most modest of modest graves and the easiest to pass by, for there was nothing remotely grand about it. It was like a tiny lozenge, of the kind sacred to the memory of Pip's five unnamed brothers, those 'exceedingly early' travellers to nowhere. He had to bend low to read the inscription Walter's father had written for his extravagant young son, Walter Landor Dickens. Walter had died on his way down from a hill station with a sudden gush of blood from his mouth. And that was the end of the youth known in his family as Young Skull because of his high cheekbones. Then, as Harry Chapman was peering at the faded letters on the gravestone, a curious thing happened. He was touched gently on the shoulder by what seemed to be a skeletal hand. He turned his head and saw the figure who was standing before him in the ward. He rose and faced the man in the frock coat, who said:

— Mr Dickens was kinder to me than he was to his sons. I am Philip Pirrip, alias Pip, by the way. And you, I assume, are Mr Harry Chapman?

— I am, was his stupefied answer.

— Mr Dickens was upset by the news of Walter's death, but not exactly overcome with grief.

He was too astonished to reply.

— There is a chop house not far from here. Would you care to join me for luncheon?

— I should be delighted.

But the delights of a lamb chop washed down with wine or beer were soon denied him, for the phantasmal Pip evaporated the very moment they were outside the cemetery. Harry Chapman was left alone with the memory of the illusion. It was, he reasoned, the heat's doing.

Pip had vanished from the hospital, too, leaving silence and darkness behind him.

He awoke to the sound of a woman moaning. She was a newcomer to the ward, for he could hear Sister Driver attempting to calm her, as she had calmed him.

— You're in safe hands, Mrs Stubbs. I'll give you something to ease the pain. There, there.

— Help me. Help me.

— Of course we'll help you. That's what we're here for.

Please keep her quiet, divine Sister Nancy, he nearly said aloud. Give her a shot of Dr Pereira's magic potion. Anything to stop that terrible noise.

Mrs Stubbs let out a shriek of Wagnerian intensity, piercing enough to quell any dragon or demon.

— She has to be taken to theatre straight away, said a voice, not Dr Pereira's. — We must operate within the hour.

— Yes, Professor.

— Otherwise – well, you know what I mean by 'otherwise'.

A mild commotion ensued. Harry Chapman listened as the newly arrived Mrs Stubbs was newly removed from his proximity. He reminded himself to ask Sister Nancy what, precisely, was wrong with the unseen, unknown woman.

— Curiosity killed the cat, remarked his mother, the deflating cliché at her imperious command. — Trust you to want to find out the worst.

The worst, he had once tried to explain to her, during his tormented adolescence – the worst time in life to explain anything of seriousness to anyone – is what being human is finally about. How arrogant and unfeeling he was then, in true Philip Pirrip fashion, in his assumption that Alice Chapman was indifferent to suffering. He had tried, in the year of her death, to make it clear to her that he appreciated the love for him she had never been able to express in simple terms. Her meals, he reasoned, offered sufficient evidence of the unspoken affection she felt for her children.

— Love? Affection? Meals? What on earth are you saying?

What on earth, indeed. Why had he bothered? He

remembered, now, that she had always scoffed at love scenes in films and television dramas.

— Look at the fools, she'd sneer. — Just look at them.

— They're only acting, Mum, Jessie would remind her.
— They're pretending.

— They're bloody idiots, whatever they're doing.

What kind of courtship did Frank Chapman and Alice Bartrip have? The question was still pertinent, given his mother's lasting contempt for even fictional displays of affection. Had he whispered sweet nothings in her ear? Had they gazed longingly into each other's eyes? Had they invented, as lovers do, their own private terms of endearment? Had he bought her, on his meagre earnings, chocolates and flowers? It was hard for him to imagine them ever enjoying a sweet romance, for when he, Harry Chapman, was just a small boy his parents were exhibiting crabbiness whenever they were together, finding excuses to be at one another's throats.

— The little you know, Harry, of what your father felt for me.

Yes, the little he knew was precious little: that they'd held hands at the pictures; that they'd spent Sunday afternoons in summer lolling in deckchairs and listening to the brass band in Hyde Park; that they'd gone out to eat jellied eels and mashed potatoes each Friday night. That was as much as he knew of their wooing.

— Mr Chapman?

He was being addressed by a male nurse, whose name he deciphered, in the muted light, as Maciek Nazwisko.

— You wish pass water, sir?

— Why not?

— Sir?

— Yes, I wish to pass water.

So he passed water, filling to within overflowing the bottle Nurse Nazwisko held for him.

— You had need, Mr Chapman.

— Yes, I did.

— You will OK be till morning?

— I hope I will.

— I take away.

— Thank you.

— Sleep your best sleep.

Was that, he wondered, a Polish saying in a literal translation, or simply Maciek Nazwisko's own peculiar expression? Either way, the notion of a best sleep pleased him.

He was drifting off when a young woman, dressed in the high-waisted style of the French Empire, appeared.

— I have a bone to pick with you, Mr Chapman.

— Who the hell are you?

— Your language is intemperate. I am Emma Woodhouse, whom you had the temerity to impersonate fifty-six years ago in an impossibly inadequate – not to say, lamentable – adaptation of the novel mostly concerned, and quite properly, with myself. You were a boy of fourteen in that school performance. What could you have ascertained of my character, a child such as you were from an impoverished background? Not a great amount, I wager. Such presumption.

— I did my best for you. The older members of the audience were most appreciative. They were shocked when I – I mean you – was and were patronisingly rude to poor verbose Miss Bates.

— Tell that bossy cow where to get off, said Alice Chapman, interrupting the conversation with her usual acerbity.

— Who is that vulgar, shrewish creature, Mr Chapman?

— My mother. My cockney Clytemnestra.

— I recollect that your Harriet Smith had a common accent also.

— Bobby? I've forgotten the sound of his voice.

— I have not, Mr Chapman. I have decidedly not forgotten his coarse vowels.

He was debating whether to ask if she were still married to the priggish Mr Knightley when Nancy Driver arrived to wish him goodnight.

— Are you comfortable, Harry?

— You know I'm not. How could I be, Sister?

— Don't fret. Dr Pereira's on your case. He'll make a decision tomorrow, I'm sure.

— I hate being unwell.

— Everyone does.

— There you're wrong, Nancy. Just think of Emma Woodhouse's father.

— Who?

— I'm sorry. He's in a book, but he's all too real. He's a professional invalid, you might say.

— Oh, yes. I've dealt with some of those.

— How is Mrs Stubbs?

— Mrs Stubbs, Harry?

— The woman who was here a short while ago. She was screaming with pain.

— She's not out of the woods yet, but we hope she soon will be. I can't say more.

Did he want her to say more? Did he really wish to learn that Mrs Stubbs, she of the moaning and the Brünnhilde shriek, was in a much worse physical condition than Harry Chapman?

— Let me know what happens to her. Tell me if and when she gets out of the woods.

Was this the best sleep he was sleeping? It didn't seem like it. He would complain to Maciek Nazwisko should he appear tomorrow with the obliging bottle. This was decidedly not the best sleep he had ever slept – in point of boring fact, it was actually one of the very worst. The dream he was currently dreaming was totally devoid of interest. He almost longed for a guest appearance by Alice Chapman in full, malignant flow. Where was the Duchess of Bombay when he really needed her? Not here, among so many shadows. Nobody lively was waiting on the dim horizon. He was asking himself if he were dead the second he awoke.

— Am I dead?

— Of course you aren't, replied a voice he didn't recognise from somewhere in the ward. — What a stupid thing to say.

He thanked the stranger for clarifying the matter with her prompt response.

— Don't thank me for stating the obvious.

— Are you Mrs Stubbs, by any chance?

— No, I'm not. Why should I be?

— She was here earlier today, in a wretched state.

— Sorry, Mr Undecided-Whether-He's-Living-Or-Dead, but I am not in a wretched state. For your information, I am only moderately unwell.

— You sound very chirpy.

— Chirpy? Me? Needs must, as they say. No point in being miserable, is there?

— No, I don't suppose there is.

— What are you in for?

— I wish I knew.

— They haven't told you anything?

— Not yet.

— Well, goodnight to you, anyway.

— Goodnight.

Oh my, the old Adam, the original sinner, was stirring down below.

— This is not the time or the place, he instructed his penis. — Stop misbehaving.

He couldn't be in absolute physical decline, he assured himself. One part of him, at least, was in working order.

Monday

HE PLAYED HIS first, and last, major Shakespearean
role when he was fifteen. To Harry Chapman's surprise
and dismay, he had been cast as the King in *King Henry the
Fourth, Part One*, a monarch who – on first acquaintance
with the text – seemed to do little more than sit on his
throne and give voice to his manifold dissatisfactions, chief
of which was the unruly behaviour of his son and heir, Prince
Hal. It was only in rehearsals that he realised that Henry's
justified melancholy spoke to his very soul. So impressed
was the producer, Mr Oliver, by the broody power of young
Chapman's interpretation that he gave him an extra soliloquy to deliver – the sombre lines from *Part Two* in which
the King, in his nightgown, laments his inability to sleep.
His lowest, lowliest subjects in their 'smoky cribs', on their
'uneasy pallets', have the gift denied him in his perfumed
chamber – the temporary forgetfulness which sleep affords.

In the course of his doleful ruminations, Henry summons
up an image of a ship-boy on the 'high and giddy mast',
sent up by the captain and crew to signal warning of storms
or other dangers. Yet sleep, despite the prospect of rough
winds and 'ruffian billows', could 'seal up the ship-boy's
eyes' unwittingly, even as it refuses to do so for his older and
tired ones in the palace at Westminster. Harry Chapman

was haunted instantly by the thought of the boy in the crow's nest, and pictured him shinning up the pole to keep watch.

There he was – a grey wig covering his mousy locks; a grey beard stuck to his chin with glue; a vast gold robe filling out his skinny frame – looking as like a king as it was possible for a dustman's son to look. Inside that robe, shorn of the wig and beard, he more resembled the ship-boy of his own imagining. He called his alter ego Jack, as befitted a sailor. The years passed and Harry Chapman put on weight, and his mousy locks became pepper-and-salt and then white, but Jack remained lithe and alert, his eyes – when not sealed up – ever more vigilant for the tempests to come. Jack had accompanied Harry to Italy, America, India, Egypt, Australia, in dreams and reveries and in those frequent moments when the lad's imaginer felt trepidation about the future.

— Harry, I have fears for you.

— What fears, Jack?

— There are dark clouds looming over yonder.

— It is kind of you to warn me.

Those clouds, sighted by Jack, foretold the last illness of his companion of twenty years, his friend and enemy encased in the same flesh. No one had manifested the tyranny of love with such dedication to terrible duty as Christopher, who needed to be adored and hated, his relish for adoration and hatred being about equal.

— I love you, said Christopher to Harry, and Harry, who had never heard the three words spoken with such conviction, was in no doubt that he believed him.

— Thank you.

— I will say it again, Harry. I love you. Have I made my feelings clear?

— You have.

— So you've got the message?

— Yes, Christopher.

— You won't get a better offer.

— Won't I?

— Absolutely not. You can rely on me. I love you, Harry.

Christopher's fiercely concentrated eyes, Harry noticed, were green. He could see them now, in the ward, separated from their owner, looking down on his helplessness.

— I loved you, Harry.

Love? What was love, in the gospel according to the unsaintly Christopher? It was all to do with possession, with the ownership of the green eyes; it was to do with Harry, the talented young author, whom he had to have for himself entirely, body and soul, soul and body, the two for ever indistinguishable. That was Christopher's notion of love.

He caught himself weeping, as he so often did these days. The old weep. The old shed tears for unaccountable reasons, for scenes and circumstances buried somewhere inside them, for words said or unsaid, for the very fact of their being born.

— Oh, Harry dear, whatever's the matter?

It was Nancy Driver asking the concerned question, gently as always.

— I've no idea, Sister Nancy. I've no idea at all.

— Don't be afraid. Dr Pereira will be here shortly.

He suddenly remembered Mrs Stubbs and her Wagnerian screaming, and wondered if she was out of the woods.

— She's doing fine. She'll survive.

— There was another woman here, late last evening. She had a very cheerful voice. She said she was moderately unwell. Is she still in the ward?

— No, Harry. You are an intelligent man, so let me tell you the truth. She died in the night, while you were asleep.

— Did she?

— She wasn't moderately unwell, and bless her for saying she was. She was quite beyond help.

— What was her name?

— Why do you wish to know?

— Curiosity. We had a conversation. I'd have liked to talk to her again.

— Iris Gibson. Mrs Iris Gibson. A widow.

— My son's a typical nosy parker, Alice Chapman declared from her movable nowhere.

— How old was she, Nancy?

— A bit older than you.

— You'll be next, my so-called son. You mark my words.

— Seventy-three, to be precise.

Mrs Gibson had spoken to him eight times, if he remembered correctly. Was this loss he was feeling now? Hardly, for he hadn't seen her and was ignorant of her past. Yet a certain quality in her tone of voice – caustic, but sanely so, and not to be compared to his mother's cruel sarcasm – lingered with him. She'd assured him, jokingly, that he wasn't dead a mere hour or two before she'd joined the ever-increasing majority. He hadn't thanked her sufficiently for that assurance.

— You've stopped crying.

Yes, he had. He smiled faintly at Sister Nancy, who was beaming down on him.

— Your blood pressure's normal, Harry. No problems there.

Ah, good, good, he thought. That's something to celebrate.

— I can see mischief in your eyes.

— You're shrewd, Nancy Driver.

The mad idea came to him that if he had to stay long in this hell then Sister Driver could be the Virgil to his Dante, his guide to the lost souls and enfeebled bodies trapped, or imprisoned, inside. He was grinning now.

— Share the joke with me, Harry.

Would his new-found Virgil, clearly not an expert on the rudiments of farming and a very unlikely chronicler of the Trojan Wars, appreciate the role he had allotted her?

— I have silly ideas from time to time, Nancy.

— You need a sense of humour in this place. That's the one thing that's always very welcome.

— I would echo that sentiment, said Dr Pereira, who had appeared behind her. — I seem to be interrupting a happy conversation.

Harry looked at the man he already accounted his curly-headed saviour and marvelled at his beauty. Oh, to be young again and healthy; to function in a society that contained this Spanish Scot, this Scottish Spaniard.

— I'm afraid I must strike a serious note, Mr Chapman.

— Must you?

— Yes. Your recent blood test shows that you haven't been taking proper care of yourself. Your liver, in particular, has received an unnecessary amount of damage.

— I only drink superior wines.

— To excess, sometimes, perhaps?

— Sometimes.

Unlike Christopher, he might have said, who drank gin round the clock in his last years. There was the aubade gin, the breakfast gin, the elevenses gin, the lunchtime glug, the teatime pickup, the dinner of clear liquid and a mouth-ful of meat or salad, and then the nightcap, the tranquilliser

41

that ensured the terror, for Harry, of vicious reproaches, which would be unacknowledged ('I never, never said that') as dawn declared itself.

— I know, Dr Pereira, that – compared with some – I am a moderate drinker.

— Not moderate enough, Mr Chapman.

— I should very much like you to call me Harry.

— I think I can oblige you on that score.

— Please do.

— Have you ever had an endoscopy, Mr Chapman? I'm sorry. Harry.

— No, I haven't.

— You will have one this afternoon. You are aware of what's involved?

— Yes.

— It's a routine affair, really.

And with that reassurance, if such it was, the doctor departed. His suburban Virgil was joined now by Marybeth Myslawchuk and an owlish student nurse who was introduced to him as Philip Warren.

— We're going to change your bedlinen, Harry. Perhaps you'd care to entertain us with a poem while we labour on your behalf.

— You should have given me notice, Marybeth.

— No excuses.

The three of them lifted him up carefully and placed him in the armchair that had yet to accommodate Harry Chapman's first visitor.

— What's it to be about? Love?

— Love will do just fine.

— Is love fine for you, Philip Warren?

The youth blushed and nodded and giggled.

— Then love it is.

But whose love, and when, and where? Ah yes, the young cleric, the future Reverend Giles Fletcher, that all-too-brief celebrator of boundless lust – yes, the otherwise pious Giles had the right words for his attentive trio.

— This is a Wooing Song, ladies and gentleman, also known as 'The Enchantress's Song'. It comes from a longer work, *Christ's Victorie and Triumph*, dating from 1610, when the poet would have been twenty-three or twenty-four. Here goes, amigos.

> *Love is the blossom where there blows*
> *Every thing that lives or grows:*
> *Love doth make the Heav'ns to move,*
> *And the Sun doth burn in love;*
> *Love the strong and weak doth yoke,*
> *And makes the ivy climb the oak,*
> *Under whose shadows lions wild,*
> *Soften'd by love, grow tame and mild . . .*

He stopped and remarked that the best was about to come. But he stayed silent.

— Have you forgotten the words, Harry?
— God forbid. Of course I haven't.
— It would be understandable, given your –
— Given my what, Marybeth? My illness? My age? Keep listening.

> *Love no med'cine can appease,*
> *He burns the fishes in the seas:*
> *Not all the skill his wounds can stench,*
> *Not all the sea his fire can quench . . .*

— Is that it, Harry?
— There's a bit more, but I think you've heard enough.

Giles lived a further thirteen years, dying of malaria in his Suffolk parish. His wife, who may or may not be the enchantress, quickly remarried. Her second husband was also a clergyman, but he didn't write poems. Here endeth today's lesson.

— Thank you. What are we going to do for poetry when you leave?

— A good question, Nancy.

'Leave' – he liked the idea of leaving the hospital; alive, of course. She'd used the word casually, as a matter of certain fact. She wasn't implying that he'd leave in a box, ready for either earth or fire.

— I'm the only person of my acquaintance with a large repertoire of remembered poetry. But there must be other fanatics around.

— We'll look out for them, Harry, said Marybeth Myslawchuk. — If they exist, we'll track them down.

They returned him to the bed – his trap; his freshly laundered prison. He saw that Sister Driver was staring pointedly at the empty chair.

— You must have friends, Harry.

— Plenty.

— Give me their names and phone numbers.

— I would prefer not to, Sister Nancy. I don't want them to see me like this.

— You don't look so very terrible.

— And you are kind, Nurse.

— Think of their feelings, Harry.

— That's precisely what I'm doing. Have you had word from Graham?

— Not yet.

— He, and nobody else, must be told I'm here.

— Well, Harry, your perverse wish is our command.

Harry Chapman had, in truth, many lovely friends, women mostly. One, especially, had been his bemused and amusing confidante for – oh God, how long was it? – fifty-three years. They had met when they were both training for the stage, and time hadn't dimmed the qualities they had detected in one another almost at first meeting. Cynicism can be afforded warm and generous expression, and Pamela's brand of world-weariness, on the lips of a twenty-year-old, sounded as wise to him then as it did now. Pamela had never abandoned acting, as he had, and appeared irregularly in television dramas, as benign or disgruntled grandmothers, elderly spinsters, dying or not dying in hospital wards where the staff were as much occupied with their rampant sexual cravings as they were with the welfare of their unfortunate patients. Pamela had died twice in the popular Saturday-evening medical saga – as Ernesta Abercrombie, a forthright lesbian novelist, famous for her wartime epic *Cry God for Harriet*, and Lady Sybil Clough-Bagshawe, a fox-hunting country gentlewoman with a son and daughter eager to learn of an inheritance the viewers know she has already bequeathed to an animal charity. To these ill-written roles, Pamela brought an understated dignity, a refusal to indulge in easy caricature that transcended the superficiality of the material.

— You've gone very silent, his Virgil observed. — Are you having second thoughts, Harry?

— No.

— You should have married that Pamela, chipped in the oracular Alice. — That's what I advised you to do when you invited her over for Sunday dinner. She was sensible and practical, despite her being an actress. But did you take my advice?

The question, like most of her questions, was rhetorical.

— No, you didn't, she continued. — You could have settled down with Pamela and raised a family, but you had to be different, as was your wont. Then you chose to have that Christopher rule your life.

— It was Christopher who nicknamed you Clytemnestra —

— Who's she when she's at home?

This Clytemnestra's Argos was south London — the mean, poky streets between the gasworks and the candle factory — and her Agamemnon, her general-in-chief, with his lordly dust cart, was called Frank. If there was an Aegisthus in the district, her demon costermonger lover, he was a phantom, a figment of her constricted imagination, for no one ever saw him. It was safe to assume that Frank wasn't murdered by Alice and the invisible Aegisthus, but had succumbed to pneumonia along with hundreds of others that bleak, fog-bound November. Harry, at the age of eleven, was no vengeful Orestes, regardless of the taunts from Alice that caused him to harbour murder in his innermost heart, and Jessie — mourn her beloved father though she did — was not cut out to be a scheming Electra. No, the top half of number 96 could not be accounted a house fit for the Atreus family, and Frank's long-dead brother — a pretend Menelaus in the guise of Sidney, and an occasional burglar of magisterial incompetence — had left a widow named Mabel, whose puckered lips had sunk a thousand schooners of sweet sherry in the snug bar of the King's Head and had fired the topless towers of Ilium with many a belch and a bibulous apology for her bad manners.

— Sweet Helen, make me immortal with a kiss, he said now, picturing the obliging Mabel, her nylon blouse in disarray, on the last occasion he had seen her, cheerfully maudlin.

— Who's Helen? asked Marybeth Myslawchuk. — Do you want her to visit you?

— Her phone's been disconnected, he replied. — If you dial Ilium 1234, you'll get no sound at all.

— He's up to his mischief, Marybeth. 'Ilium 1234' – what nonsense he's coming out with.

— You don't need to remind me, Sister. I swear he was coming out with nonsense the moment he learned to talk.

That was another of Alice Chapman's beliefs – that her son, enslaved by the power of his imagination, lived in a ridiculous universe that defied sense and credibility. Harry was destined to stay on Planet Make-Believe all his born days, despite her best efforts to bring him down to earth.

— Harry dear, take no notice of my sister.

— Auntie Rose.

— Yes, my sweetheart, I'm in the vicinity. God knows quite where, but I'm in the building, far away enough from Malice for comfort.

Rose, his beauteous aunt, the impossible optimist, the detector of goodness in those who hid it from everyone, including themselves, was at hand at last, after a long absence from his thoughts.

— It's wonderful to hear from you.

— I fancy you'd begun to forget me, Harry.

— Never, Auntie. It's just that –

— It's just that your mother has to have her say. Isn't that so?

— Yes.

— The last word has to be hers. Even when it's the wrong one, as it usually is. But she has her good side, Harry, though she doesn't often care to show it. You're a writer, as I shouldn't have to remind you. She needs your understanding, especially now.

— Is that Helen you're talking to, Harry?

— No, Nancy. I'm just muttering to myself.

— They say that's the first sign of madness, ventured Philip Warren, smiling.

— *They* say a lot of things, Master Philip Warren. They seldom stop saying things. *They* have been commenting on human nature since time immemorial. Their tongues will wag until the end of the world.

— Don't mock the boy, Harry.

— Oh, I'm not mocking him. I've been mad for aeons, Nancy. The first sign came long, long before Philip was born.

His unspoken wish to be alone was soon granted. He was to be examined later in the day – Dr Pereira hadn't revealed exactly when – and must stay calm and hopeful. He wasn't quite sure why he had to do so, but calmness and hopefulness seemed a better proposition than anxiety.

— What's looming, Jack? he enquired of the ship-boy.

Jack cleared his perpetually young throat, as if to suggest that words of either warning or comfort were presently beyond his powers.

Harry Chapman, you really are mad, he thought to himself, and then Jack, high up on his mast, responded:

— Be of good cheer, Captain. The shore's in sight.

What could the boy, the skinny urchin, mean?

And the image of skinniness, of being pigeon-chested, of having a body already weakened by a near-fatal illness in infancy, came to the seventy-year-old Harry Chapman, lying powerless in his hospital bed. He was twelve again, and attempting to learn to swim, and horribly conscious of his meagre physique. His instructor, Mr Sampson, pushed him into the pool at the deep end and dared him not to drown by using his arms and legs as Nature dictated. Nature took a few frightening minutes to dictate to Harry his best means of survival, but survive he did, finding himself at last in the shallow end, where he stood up, gasping and gasping for breath.

The baths had been built in the declining years of the nineteenth century, and were designed in the Gothic mode. He looked down at the tiled floor of the pool and saw that, in his fear, he had yellowed the water. Then, climbing the four or five steps that led to safety, he had to cover his eyes to protect them from the glare of the fierce sunlight reflected in the high window. On that May afternoon in 1949, he might have been in a cathedral instead of the public baths with a swimming pool that reeked of chlorine. Temporarily blinded by sun and glass, he turned and was blinded a second time by a sight that would never leave him. He was dazzled, nothing less than dazzled, by a blond youth standing nonchalantly, hand on hip, in the doorway of a cubicle. The eighteen-year-old, who was soon to leave the school and join the army, was called David Cooke. The vision of David Cooke, in his blue trunks, excited and depressed the silent worshipper who was Harry Chapman. David's teeth were wonderfully even and white, like a film star's, and that in itself was a miracle in England in the 1940s, when dentistry was a practice that terrified rich and poor alike. His perfectly shaped body was bronzed, whereas Harry's was ghostly pale. Almost two decades later, in the Accademia in Florence, Harry Chapman, now the author of a successful, prize-winning novel, stood before the David of Michelangelo and thought of the David brought into radiant being by Mr and Mrs Cooke in a smart London suburb in 1931. Had he retained, at thirty-eight, his glowing youthfulness? Or had military service, marriage and fatherhood aged him? Was he indistinguishable these days from the other middle-class men setting off each morning to earn steady wages in order to support their wives and children?

Was his body still in proportion, or did he have a well-fed Englishman's pot belly?

— You were just as lovely once, he told the real David while seeming to address Michelangelo's eternal, uncircumcised second King of the Hebrews.

Unanswerable questions then; unanswerable questions now. What was certain in 1949, and as certain in 1968, was that David Cooke, a king of sorts to be regarded with awe and admiration, was not available, either as friend or lover, to the Harry Chapmans who considered themselves blessed if His Majesty honoured them with a smile or a nod acknowledging their inadequate existence. The ridiculous truth was that Harry's reverence for David Cooke and his kind never progressed to lust or desire – and the lasting evidence of that truth was demonstrated on a university campus in a desolate part of America when Harry Chapman was approached by a freshman named Duane, of pure Nordic stock, whose gift for English did not begin to equal his lauded talent for basketball. Duane was not the brightest of Dr Chapman's students, but he seemed amiably gauche and caused no problems in class. His grades were low, as were those of his fellow jocks, whose interests didn't extend beyond sport, girls, TV and beer.

The preoccupied Dr Chapman was walking slowly back to his apartment on a muggy April evening – summer had followed winter, not spring, as it sometimes did in the north-west – when a car drew up alongside him, and a voice said:

— Hi, Dr Chapman. Can I drop you off some place?

— Oh, hello, Duane. That's very kind of you.

So Duane – at the wheel of his dad's vast Chevrolet – drove his teacher to the neat apartment he shared with a woman of Italian origin who was visiting relatives in Boston.

— Would you like to come in? I'm going to cook pasta, and you're welcome to join me.

Duane accepted the invitation unhesitatingly.

— You'll have to be patient while I prepare my special bolognese sauce.

— Sounds good.

Harry Chapman offered Duane a glass of Chianti, but the youth said he'd be happier with a Michelob, if Dr Chapman had one. Yes, Dr Chapman could oblige, and brought out a can from the refrigerator.

Duane settled himself in the dining area.

— Cheers, Dr C. You English guys say 'Cheers', yeah?

— That's right. Cheers, Duane.

— You're a great guy, you know that?

— I don't know that, but thank you for the compliment.

Harry Chapman, to his considerable amazement, was pleased to have Duane's company. They wouldn't be discussing Shakespeare or Melville or Dickens, or any literature at all, and that didn't bother him in the least. He listened contentedly as Duane informed him that some were born to be sportsmen and others, no disrespecting Dr Chapman, were better in the brain department.

— And I belong in the brain department. Is that correct, Duane?

— You sure do.

— I've been there too long, Duane. The brain department, that is.

— Well, that's how the cookie crumbles, wouldn't you say?

— I would. Definitely. I would.

They sat down to eat *tagliatelle alla bolognese* and a crisp green salad.

— This looks so good, Dr Chapman.

— Call me Harry, Duane. Just for tonight.

— If that's OK, Dr Chapman.

— Of course it is.

Harry Chapman felt no desire for the beautiful specimen sitting opposite him, whose resemblance to the David
Cooke of thirty years past became more pronounced with
each sip of wine. Duane explained the rules of basketball
to him, passing on the information as though to a child,
and Harry revelled in the young man's earnestness. Duane
consumed four cans of beer during dinner, and another two
as they sat in front of the television watching the national
and local news bulletins. Harry opened a second bottle, and
Duane winked at him roguishly as he pulled out the cork
and sniffed it.

— My folks were sure sore at that last grade you gave
me, Harry.

— It was a C plus, wasn't it?

— Minus, Harry.

— If you work a bit harder this semester and take care
over your spelling and grammar, then things are bound to
improve, he heard himself lying.

— Easier said than done.

— Do it for your parents, Duane.

— Where's the bathroom, Harry?

— Second door on the left.

Duane was a proud pisser, to judge by the noise he made.
Harry went into the kitchen area and began to put the
plates, the knives and forks, the dessert and salad bowls
into the dishwasher. He rinsed each object under the tap
first, as was his pernickety custom. When he had finished,
he returned to the sitting room. The television was still on,
but there was no sign of his guest.

— Duane?

The bathroom door was open; his bedroom door closed.

— Duane? Are you in there?

— Uh-huh.

— Are you all right?

— Hunky-dory. Come and see.

What he saw ought to have made him delirious, for Duane was spread out on his bed – naked, except for a pair of blue shorts carefully lowered to reveal brownish pubic hair and a would-be enticing fraction of his penis. His tanned body was truly a marvel of symmetry, worthy to be sculpted by Michelangelo or Donatello. Dr Chapman stared at the grinning Duane with obvious approval.

— You like what you see, Harry?

— Yes, David.

— Who the fuck's David? It's Duane.

— I'm sorry, Duane. You remind me of someone I knew long ago.

Duane sat up and slipped out of his shorts. Harry Chapman ought to have been ecstatic, overcome with lust, but he couldn't be, he simply couldn't be.

— Have you had enough to eat, Harry?

— Yes.

— The answer's no. You fags – no disrespect – are always hungry.

He ate what Duane plunged into his mouth, and oh, it was an interminable, uncomfortable meal. He feared for his new fillings. The boisterous Duane let out cries of 'Yeah, yeah, yeah' and 'Oh God' and 'This is great head' and Harry, aware that the prey he was feeding on was in the early stages of drunkenness, knew that the inevitable explosion would happen later rather than sooner. He munched and munched and licked and licked and prayed for Duane to emit the yelp of pleasure that usually accompanied the moment of bliss, and then he was swallowing Duane's seed – biblically speaking – and almost choked but coughed and spluttered instead.

After a silence, Duane said quietly:

— You just had what hundreds of chicks would die for.

— Thank you, Duane.

But no expression of gratitude came from the baseball titan, who dressed quickly.

— That deserves a higher grade, wouldn't you say, Harry?

Harry, unable to answer in the affirmative, nodded.

— Think about it.

He thought about it for most of the night, accounting himself a colossal fool. He should have told Duane he wasn't remotely attracted to him, except in a purely aesthetic sense. Aesthetic? It was unlikely that Duane was acquainted with the term. He cursed his idiocy, but wisdom after the event was no consolation.

— That was disgusting, Harry Chapman – what little I could make of it, which wasn't very much, I thank my lucky stars. To think a son of mine could stoop to such things beggars belief. You need to wash your filthy mind out with soap and water.

— Oh, I've done worse things, Mother.

— Are you awake, Harry?

— Nancy?

— The same. You'll be having your endoscopy at three thirty. Mr Russell will be in charge. He's an expert.

— What time is it?

— Just after two.

— Will this expert discover what's wrong with me?

— Yes. Yes, Harry, he will. I'm confident.

That's what he wanted to hear from his soft-spoken Virgil.

— If you're confident, Nancy Driver, I am.

— Well said, Harry.

His mother, so incurious about the important concerns in her Harry's life while she was living, invited him now to tell her of those worse things he had done.

— Go on, Harry. Shock me.

— You're dead.

— So what? I'm still shockable.

He begged her not to stray out of character, but even as he did so he recalled with what disdainful pleasure she consumed the contents of the Sunday newspaper referred to by his father as either *The Barmaids' Bible* or *The Whores' Gazette*. She would click her tongue to indicate disapproval, and mouth the word 'disgusting' as she went on reading. The news item that shocked her most involved a Chinese hypnotist employed in a bacon factory who used his 'diabolical skills' the better to seduce the female slicer operators under his command. He would send the unwary girls into a deep sleep and then take 'evil liberties' in his private office. Alice Chapman said she was appalled by his cunning, and cut out the lengthy report of his antics to show to her friends over tea and walnut cake.

— You can't trust a Chink, she declared as a matter of undeniable fact.

— Why is that, Mother?

— It's the eyes.

— What about them?

— They look sideways, not straight ahead.

— Sideways or not, he managed to hypnotise six women.

— He wouldn't have put a spell on me, however hard he tried. I'd have sent him packing the moment he cast his slitty eyes on me. Which is what those women should have done.

— Yes, Mother.

— The silly cows.

In March 1950, David Cooke was somewhere else – in Korea, perhaps – serving his country. There was no one left in the school who could be deemed an Adonis or a Greek athlete. On a blustery day that March, Harry Chapman and ten other thirteen-year-olds ran a mile race, which necessitated circling the school playground eight times. He finished a creditable fourth, and loved long-distance running thereafter. The afternoon ended with the sweaty contestants taking a shower, amid accusations of 'Jew boys'. Harry Chapman, who had been circumcised on the very day of his birth for entirely medical reasons, was only a pretend Jew, but Leo Duggan was genuinely and unashamedly Jewish.

Their mockers each had a 'Coliseum curtain' (as Christopher insisted on labelling the foreskin) which had to be pulled back to reveal what Harry and Leo kept on permanent display. They were different, and it showed.

— Harry's no Yid, but Leo Duggan is, said Ralph Edmunds, who had established himself already as an intimidating bully.

Leo made no response, continuing to lather himself with the coarse soap that was considered good for the complexion.

— It's not just his prick, it's his conk as well. It's like a bleeding hook. You could open a tin with it.

Harry Chapman wanted to speak up for the still-silent Leo, to defend him from the taunts of Ralph Edmunds and his gang, but the words of rebuke stayed in his head. The hirsute Ralph looked older than his years, and Harry, watching him assert his brutish authority, experienced a sensation that shocked and frightened the platonic worshipper of David Cooke. His blood raced, his heart quickened, and he recognised what he had only read about or seen in films at the Super Palace. He imagined his whole miserable body – not just his face, which he could sense was blushing – turning red with lust. This was shocking enough, but it was the ache of hunger, an ache deep in the pit of his stomach, that terrified him. It was a new kind of pain to him, and he suspected that it might be the prelude to a new kind of pleasure, too.

— Why are you shaking, Harry? Do I scare you, skinny boy?

— No, Ralph.

— Liar. I scare you. Yes, I do.

He moved close to Harry Chapman, the swot of the class, and took the wet, shaking, lust-inflamed creature into his own wet, hairy arms. He gave the boy from the brain department a bear hug, and Ralph's eight cronies laughed and whooped their approval. Harry struggled to be free, while hoping that the clutch would contain him always. He was damned now, he thought; he was among the lost.

— Let me go.

— Let you go, Harry?

— You're hurting me.

— That's my way.

And then Harry Chapman was cast aside, discarded, and left to wonder why it was that Ralph Edmunds had squeezed him so tightly. His tormentor was smiling, showing teeth slightly stained with nicotine, and Harry, the weakling, reached for a towel to cover himself. His pretend-Jew's manhood had stiffened, much to Ralph's amusement.

— Mine's twice the size and it's soft.

— So that's what you did at school when you should have been educating yourself, said the voice that only Harry Chapman's death could silence. You filthy little sod.

He was wretched on the evening of the day of the race and for several months afterwards. He knew little of sexual matters, and that little told him his desire for the school's principal bully was unnatural and perverted. He should be chasing girls – as Ralph was, and as Leo and Bobby and all the other boys of his acquaintance were. He would wake in the middle of the night and think of being squeezed to happy breathlessness in the shower and then he had to ease his longing with his increasingly skilled right hand. The moment of blissful ejaculation achieved, there followed self-contempt and its accompaniment shame. He crawled out of bed once and went down on his knees and prayed to the God of Milton and George Herbert and John Donne to purify his soul, to erase the flesh of Ralph Edmunds from his thoughts, and to ensure that he would grow into a man who loved women.

For his was a literary God, the loving – if absent – father of Christ rather than the vengeful tyrant of the Old Testament. He was the kindly spirit encountered in Sunday services at the church in which William Blake married his illiterate young bride. Harry Chapman came out of St Mary's early one summer afternoon and lingered in the churchyard. Some of the blackened graves dated back two centuries, and he had to look hard to decipher the names of the persons buried beneath. 'Sacred to the memory of –' was a familiar refrain, but the memorialists were gone too. Thinking of this harvesting of humanity, of the good and the bad and the moderately sinful rotting together, of the invisible worms feasting, he felt a chill creep over him despite the noontide heat. Was there nothing else to expect but lasting nothingness? It would become the primary question of his life and he first asked it of himself in June 1950 and was asking it again now as he opened his eyes in the hospital ward.

— We're taking you for your endoscopy, Harry.

And now he was returned to the dull surroundings he had known for – how long was it? – two or three or, perhaps, more days. An eternity ago, he had heard the expert, Mr Russell, a stocky figure with cropped blond hair like some German general, inform his assistants that Mr Chapman needed to be anaesthetised. The patient was old and would probably resist having the instrument forced down his throat. He had to be treated gently.

That much Harry Chapman remembered, before succumbing to sleep.

— Harry? Can you hear me?

— Is that you, Dad?

— As sure as God made little apples.

— Your voice is very faint.

— I was never a loudmouth. Was I?

— No.

— I hadn't much to say to anyone after what I'd seen in the trenches.

— Tell me what you saw.

— I can't, my son.

— It's ancient history.

— Then let it be.

— You won two medals, Dad. For bravery, was it?

— It wasn't for sitting on my arse.

— You were in France for three years.

— Who told you?

— The Ministry of Defence. I wrote to them. In 1992.

— Why did you do that?

— Because you're a mystery.

— I was just an ordinary man, going about his ordinary life. There's no mystery where Frank Alfred Chapman's concerned. I was Private Number 36319. That's how important I was.

Harry Chapman had memorised the number his father was allotted after being enlisted into the Army Service Corps Regular Army on 8 December 1915. Why had he done so?

— Yes, why, Harry?

— To bring you closer, I suppose.

— What rubbish you come out with. Closer? I've been dead nigh on sixty years.

Harry begged 36319 Chapman not to be unkind to him, especially now they were reunited. They were walking on grass and surrounded by trees and bushes and the sun was warming them.

— Dad, I have to tell you something.

— You've left it late in the day.

He followed Frank's cliché with another:

— Better late than never.

— Well, son, what is it?

— Dad, I'm gay.

— I'm pleased to hear it. I'm glad you're still happy at the age you are. Seventy, isn't it?

Ah, yes. 'Gay' in the 1940s, when last they talked, had not taken on its current, widely used meaning. And besides, Harry had not known he was different in the November of 1948 when Frank ran out of breath for ever.

— Let me explain, Dad, he began, but his explanation was not forthcoming, because here was his bright-eyed Virgil removing the tubes from him and saying:

— Harry, we are going to give you some real food. It's not cordon bleu, so don't get excited.

— Not curry, I hope. I don't want a burning bum tomorrow.

— It will be light, I promise.

The meal could not have been lighter – a simple, undressed salad, with a few flecks of tuna. He ate it wolfishly. He ate it as an eremite would eat locusts.

— Was that good, Harry? asked Marybeth Myslawchuk.

— Good enough.

No Dijon mustard, no sherry vinegar, no virgin olive oil – but good enough for a starving man in a London hospital. Lettuce, tomato, cucumber and a couple of radishes. Heaven on earth, almost.

— Superb, in the circumstances.

He drank tea, as he liked it, of the weak kind described by his mother as 'gnat's piss'.

— It's as fine as champagne when you have a thirst.

— I wouldn't know, Harry. I'm a coffee fiend, me.

— What did Mr Russell find?

— You'll hear in the morning.

— Promise?

— Yes, Harry dear, we promise.

'Dear'? Where did that term of affection spring from?

— Marybeth, my dear, I have every faith in you.

— You'd better have, honey, she assured him, exaggerating her transatlantic accent. — And we all expect a poem when we come on duty. Get your brain ticking over, babe.

'Dear'? 'Babe'? He felt warm, he felt cared for suddenly, he felt strangely and temporarily at peace. He knew there were phantoms, demons, sarcastic tormentors in his midst, but at this moment, for this moment, he was as contented as any old survivor could possibly hope to be.

'Dear'? 'Babe'? Take away the question marks, and leave behind 'dear' and 'babe'. Terms of affection. These were terms he'd heard on the lips of lovers – terms he was hearing now, like soothing balm, from a plump and kindly woman, of whose existence he'd been unaware on Saturday morning. She was saying them with something close, or close enough, to conviction.

Tuesday

JOY DID NOT come in the morning to Harry Chapman, who awoke in darkness with the pain in his gut as unendurable as it had been on the afternoon of his admission to hospital. The Duchess of Bombay was still emulating Lear on the heath as the paramedics helped him into the ambulance. He'd wanted to tell them the story of her unusual life, but they had advised him to stop speaking.

— Mr Chapman? What's the trouble?

The questioner was a nurse he hadn't seen before.

— Pain.

— Whereabouts?

— In my stomach.

Which he clutched now, as if to emphasise the location.

— I'll be back in a minute.

Her minute seemed like an hour.

— I've spoken to Dr Pereira, she said. — He was a bit grumpy because he was fast asleep when I phoned him. He gave me precise instructions about what to give you.

Ah, the magic potion, the beautiful doctor's secret wonder drug.

— What's your name?

— Veronica.

— Put me out, Veronica. Put me out of this.

— I will, Mr Chapman. I promise.

She kept her promise, as he could see and feel, and soon he was in a place where pain was not even contemplated. The joyless morning was now serene afternoon or evening, it really didn't matter which. He sighed with satisfaction – the long, easeful release of breath that grants expression to deep contentment. He was at rest, at last.

— Ah, poor dear, bemoaned a fat old woman with a husky voice and a moist eye, which had a remarkable power of turning up, only showing the white of it. She was wearing a very rusty black gown, stained with snuff, and a shawl and bonnet to match. Yet she looked pleased to see him.

— He'll make a lovely corpse, she remarked to another black figure in the shadows, whom she addressed as Betsey. — He'll look lovely laid out, with a penny on each eye, afore he goes off to his long home.

The gin on her breath caused Harry Chapman to think of Christopher, who in his last years consumed it every waking hour.

— He's wandering, Betsey Prig. They all wander at the end.

— Are you Mrs Gamp? Mrs Sairey Gamp?

— You're familiar, aren't you? I am that same kindly widow woman, if it's any business of yours. The sooner you die, the sooner Mrs Prig and myself will be renumerated for our services. So hurry up, won't you?

— Don't you mean 'remunerated'?

— I mean what I say and I say what I mean and you just shut up and get ready to meet your Maker.

Jack, the ship-boy, Harry Chapman's own creation, his skin-and-bone Cassandra, jumped into view and said:

— The winds are fair for you, Master Harry. You can still set sail on the ocean of life.

— Oh, thank you, thank you, Jack.

— And come to a safe harbour.

Harry saw the child of his imagining aglow with optimism. He'd come down from the high and giddy mast, and here he was chastising the hags who wanted Harry Chapman extinct.

— You will live, Master Harry. I have no fears for you. There are no black clouds looming.

Then the skinny lad said 'Shoo' and the drunken guardians of the about-to-be-born and the soon-to-be-dead vanished, leaving the cloying perfume of raw gin behind them.

— Back to work, Master Harry. It's up the mast again for me.

— Goodbye, Jack. For the present.

After Jack had climbed out of sight, Harry Chapman tried to sleep, although he seemed to be asleep already. He certainly wasn't awake, for there were no nurses at hand and no equipment in the vicinity. Veronica's promised temporary oblivion was not to be his, it seemed.

— No rest for the wicked, sneered Alice Chapman, predictable as ever.

— I wish you would use words correctly – dead, burnt and buried as you are. I am not wicked, though I have been cruel on occasions, in common with most of the human race.

— It was only a manner of speaking, Mr Clever-Dick, Mr Know-It-All.

— And your manner of speaking was always, always dismissive of hope and promise.

His hope; his promise. These were things she'd been intent on dashing. Oh, why was he bothering with her taunts? Why was he allowing himself to remember them?

— Leave the boy alone, he heard Aunt Rose tell her sister. — Just leave him be to get on with his life.

Then there was silence, which was the one thing he craved. He listened to it, as one sometimes listens to perfect quiet, marvelling at its power to comfort. He wanted to listen into eternity, to have no further distraction. Yes, that was definitely what he wanted.

A phone rang somewhere, on and on. The ringing ceased, only to be resumed a moment later.

— Hello?

The person who picked up the receiver sounded strangely like himself.

— Are you feeling better, Harry?

— Yes, I think I am.

— That is good to hear.

— Who are you?

The caller hesitated, coughed, and answered:

— It isn't of any importance who I am.

— Why?

— Because it isn't, Harry.

— I can't put a face to you.

— You have no need to do so.

— You're not English, are you?

— No. But you have read my story in English, since you do not speak Russian. Or perhaps you are acquainted with me in French? I was a popular figure in Parisian intellectual circles in the 1890s.

— You must be my dear friend Prince Lyov Nikolayevitch Myshkin.

— Yes, Harry, I am he.

— Your voice is as I imagined it – quiet and reasonable and endlessly concerned and kind.

— I do not wish to be flattered.

66

— I have loved you since I first encountered you – on the train from Warsaw to Petersburg – when I was seventeen. I took you everywhere with me, on London trains and buses, in parks, in the lavatory, at home, on visits to friends – yes, yes, Prince Myshkin, anywhere and everywhere. When I first left you at the end of July 1954, you were back in Dr Schneider's clinic in Switzerland with a 'permanent derangement of the intellect' brought on by Rogozhin's murder of Nastasya Filippovna. The second time I met you, five years later, I hoped and prayed that your life would take a different course.

— That was sweetly silly of you, Harry.

There was a clicking sound on the line, then silence. Harry Chapman wondered how Myshkin, even in Dr Schneider's expensive and celebrated clinic, had access to the telephone. When was it invented? The 1870s, wasn't it? And when was *The Idiot* written? Think, think. The 1860s, he supposed.

— When did *The Idiot* appear? he asked Sister Nancy, who was waking him gently.

— The idiot, Harry? There's an idiot born every day, in my experience. Idiots appear wherever you look. Which particular idiot do you have in mind?

His Virgil was failing him, and he smiled at the thought.

— No matter, Nancy.

— How are you feeling?

— I was in pain earlier this morning, very bad pain. I can't feel anything now.

— We should have some news for you today.

— Good? Bad?

— It's not for me to say. Dr Pereira and Mr Russell will be able to tell you. I'm hoping good, if that's any consolation.

— Thank you.

— I'll leave you to decide which poem you're going to give us, Harry.

— Poem? Oh, yes. I'll rack what Dr Pereira's drugs have left of my brain. I will think of something. Something appropriate, perhaps, to my condition.

And what condition, precisely, was that? It could be terminal, couldn't it? He looked about him at the little he had to see in his contained surroundings. There wasn't much to stir the soul, but the will to go on living, to move again in the wide world, suddenly possessed him. He was elated. Yes, that's what he was.

— That's my lovely nephew, Aunt Rose whispered. — I lived to be ninety-seven thinking the way you're thinking. Keep going.

Could he bear the idea – yes, even the idea – of reaching ninety-seven? He doubted it. All he wanted now was to be at home with Graham, writing a book that might or might not be his last. He had never imagined attaining seventy, let alone ninety plus. Besides, poor Rose was gaga at the end, with only memories of her earliest infancy to sustain her, if that's what they did. After his final visit to her, at the Eventide Home in a tiny Sussex village, he had vowed to do what he had often contemplated doing in his tortured adolescence and beyond, should his faculties declare themselves redundant.

— I won't hear of it, Harry. Suicide's the coward's way out. Your time will come when it's good and proper and not before.

— You're going to tell me to look on the bright side, aren't you?

— I could give you worse advice.

— No, not you. That's your sister's province.

— Leave her to heaven, Harry.

68

— Yes, I will.

He had to leave her to heaven, along with Hamlet's mother Gertrude, if that's where she was. If, if: the afterlife was replete with 'ifs'. He knew, as sure as God made little apples, that she would appear to him again during his ordeal. She'd relished drama, and that relish was her terrible gift to him. How often he had tried to resist the allure of the last, coruscating word, the dramatic exit line. He could resist it now, surely, with infinity confronting him. Here was the exit of exits, and he would pass through it calmly. He found himself determined to do so.

He waited to hear her contradicting him, but for once she was blessedly silent.

— You certainly put up a fight, Harry. There, I called you Harry, said Dr Pereira. — You had to be sedated. Mr Russell didn't want to force the equipment down your throat. You fought like a demon.

— Did I? I've no memory of it.

— We discovered a lump in your stomach. It might be harmless. We shall do further exploratory tests before we decide whether or not to operate.

Harry Chapman, nodding, imagined Dr Pereira as Caravaggio's gorgeous young *Fruttaiolo* in the Borghese Gallery in Rome. The curly-haired vendor, with his exposed shoulder, is holding a basket containing black grapes, green grapes, shiny red apples, redcurrants, a blushing pear or two and a plum tomato – the whole luscious ensemble decorated with vine leaves. Gone were the doctor's white overall, his stethoscope, his doctorly demeanour, and in their glowing stead was the immortal youth with his imperishable wares.

— I like your attitude, Harry. It's good to see you smiling. I really admire your spirit.

— My spirit?

— A lesser man would have turned his face to the wall and given up hope. Stay cheerful, Harry.

And with that Dr Pereira left his spirited patient's bedside. The fruitseller lingered on for a moment or two and then followed his double out of the ward.

He was joined, soon enough, by the regular trio.

— Have you a poem for us, Harry?

— I have, Marybeth, and I haven't.

— And what exactly is that supposed to mean, honey?

— Well, there is a poem and then again there isn't.

— He's at his mischief, said Harry Chapman's Virgil.
— He enjoys his puzzles, she added with what her cockney Dante acknowledged as uncommon shrewdness.

— I shall need a little time to explain.

They gave him that precious time – Nancy Driver, Marybeth and the quizzical Philip Warren – as they changed his linen, took his temperature, checked his blood pressure and rearranged him in the bed.

He had to apologise, but this late poem of Nazim Hikmet was still working its way around his brain. It was a joyous meditation on death. He wanted to convey its message to his good friends in his own English, although it had been written in Turkish. He would tell them of the poet's life, briefly, if they had the patience to listen to him.

— We're listening, Harry.

— Where to begin?

— We can't answer that for you.

— All I need to say is that Hikmet was a devout Marxist who offended the secular state he had helped bring into being. He spent eighteen years in prison, where he wrote love letters in verse to his wife. He smoked too many cigarettes. He died, at the age of sixty-one, in Moscow, where he had lived for more than a decade. I'm going to give you Harry Chapman's version of 'My Funeral', which he wrote in April 1963.

He paused; he had to, to collect his thoughts.

— This isn't something morbid, is it, Harry?

— No, no, no. Quite the reverse. Listen. The poem begins with two questions. Will Hikmet's funeral start in the courtyard below his tiny apartment? And how will the bearers bring the coffin down three floors? The lift is too small; the stairs too narrow.

He paused a second time. Was he making any sense?

— What happens next?

— I'm coming to that, Master Philip. Laboriously, I admit. Give me a moment more.

They gave it to him, and he continued.

— *Perhaps the courtyard will be knee-deep in sunlight and*
    pigeons —

— 'Knee-deep', that's good, said Marybeth, sounding like Polonius.

— *perhaps there will be snow and children's cries mingling in*
    the air
or the asphalt glistening with rain
and the dustbins littering the place as usual . . .

— Dustbins? In a poem?

— Oh, Nancy, you disappoint me. He almost called her Virgil, the consummate chronicler of the damned.

— Dustbins are a necessity of urban life, and poetry has to address itself (Oh, he sounded so professorial) to muck, to waste, to —

— Spare us the details, Harry.
He went on.

— *If in keeping with the custom here I am to go, face open to*
  the skies,
on the hearse, a pigeon might drop something on my brow, for
  luck.
Whether a band turns up or no, children will come near me,
  children like funerals.

He stopped once more, recalling the many funerals of
his childhood: the distant relations, whose virtues were
lauded by bored and dishonest clergymen; the stillborn; the
ancients whose existence he had to take on trust, thanks to
Alice Chapman's approval or disapprobation.

— *Our kitchen window will stare after me as I go,*
  the washing in the balcony will wave to see me off.
  I have been happier here than you can ever imagine.
  Friends, I wish you all a long and happy life.

— Is that it, Harry?
— Yes. That's it.
— It's not as – how shall I call it? – it's not as *melodious*
as the others you've recited.
— I suppose it isn't. But I love the washing waving farewell to him, and the pigeon leaving the perennial message
on his brow. I find the poem curiously serene.
— You're the expert, Harry.
The expert? He was no such sterile thing. He was an
enthusiast, a hero-worshipper of those who use words or
notes or brushstrokes to convey something of the mystery
and wonder of human existence. Oh, that sounded so

high-minded, so elitist, too precious by half to explain to Nancy, Marybeth and Philip. Yet it was what he was, and what he believed, and what he would die believing – today, tomorrow, this year, next year, or in the immediate or not too distant future.

— Perhaps it's because it's in a foreign language.

— Don't worry. I've plenty more in my English poetry kitty.

Then Harry Chapman was unexpectedly sick, and the simple meal he'd been given the evening before gushed out of him. The gushing went on and on, as if he'd consumed an entire feast instead of a single plate of tuna and salad. Bowls were brought for him and borne away, and the bedclothes he'd stained removed and replaced.

— Where's it all coming from?

— That's a constant mystery, Nancy Driver assured him. — You'll feel so much better when it's over.

— When? When?

— Any minute now. Try and stay calm.

— At least the shit's coming out from somewhere.

The message NIL BY MOUTH appeared above his bed again, and the drip was attached to him – or he to the drip – once more. He saw the red blotches on his arms and knew they would increase in number as long as the pain persisted. His wounds, courtesy of Dr Pereira, the reliever of his physical suffering. His arrows.

— What day is it?

— Tuesday, Harry.

— And is that lunch being served, or dinner?

— Lunch.

— It doesn't smell enticing. Not even to a hungry soul like me.

— You're picky, honey. That's what I love about you.

Marybeth Myslawchuk kissed Harry Chapman's forehead, and he wondered on the instant if her kiss signalled his demise. Was there infinite pity in her show of affection?

— Take kindness when it's offered you.

— Yes, Auntie.

— She'll try to keep you alive, if anyone will.

— You may be right.

— Trust me.

Harry Chapman had invariably trusted her, there was no denying that, but hadn't he often been cynical about her eternal optimism? Alice's nickname for her contented sibling was 'Rosy Glow'.

— You'd think, listening to Rosy Glow, that life is a bowl of bloody cherries from start to finish. No misery, no worrying where the next penny's coming from, no aches and pains, no working till you drop, nothing but bleeding sunshine and happiness.

— Malice and myself were as different as chalk and cheese, Harry's aunt intervened. — I saw no good reason for making people more unhappy with their lot than they were already, whereas she had to twist the knife in the wound, no matter whose it was. She enjoyed preening herself at funerals, trying hard to conceal her delight that it wasn't her turn yet.

— She didn't preen herself when Dad was buried.

— No, not then, Harry dear. Not then she didn't. Just that once. She was too upset on that occasion, I grant you.

— You never married, did you, Rosy Glow? You were frightened to tie the knot. You had it easy.

— What do you know of my life, Malice?

Were they having an argument in his presence? Had Harry Chapman ever heard them quarrel? He couldn't remember. Aunt Rose's carapace, her impregnable shell of serenity, was never allowed to crack in public.

— I often fall to wondering if I chose the wrong sister, Frank Chapman said to his son as they walked briskly over the grass.

— Then you wouldn't have Jessie for a daughter and me for a son.

— That's true. But I might have had a quieter time of it with Rose. She's a stranger to moodiness.

'A stranger to moodiness' – here he was, sixty-one years later, revelling in a heartfelt phrase his laconic father had come out with on one of their Sunday walks. Harry Chapman's ears had been attuned, as long ago as 1946, to the blessed gift that even the unlettered possess of saying something peculiarly memorable. His Aunt Rose wasn't simply happy to be alive. No, no: she was 'a stranger to moodiness'.

As they neared home, and the prospect of Alice's anger at their being ten minutes late, Harry had pictured Moodiness, garbed in red and black, approaching his beloved auntie with the greeting:

— Hello, Rose Bartrip. I'm Moodiness.

— Go away. I don't wish to know you. I don't speak to strangers.

— Why are you smiling, son?

— Nothing, Dad.

— You're a funny little fellow, and no mistake.

And then Frank Chapman, in a rare display of affection, had ruffled Harry's hair.

It was a day of such intense heat that Harry Chapman, alone and palely loitering in what appeared to be a limitless desert, was desperate for the soothing comfort, however tepid it might be, of some shade. There were no trees, no bushes, to be seen. He pressed on, sweat flowing from him, his cotton shirt and trousers sticking to his tired flesh. Where was he heading? Did he have a destination? He couldn't say, in truth.

But then the questions were answered for him, with echoing voices talking excitedly of Abydos. The wind from the sea cooled Harry Chapman as he approached a throne of white marble, overlooking the city and the shore, on which was seated a bearded man he took to be no less than Xerxes, the presently triumphant king of the Persians.

— I can see the whole of my army and my navy from here, he pronounced with evident pride. — The Hellespont is hidden by my ships, and the beaches and plains of Abydos are filled with my men, and I am happy. Yes, I am happy.

Barely a moment passed before the happy king was weeping.

His uncle, Artabanus, was by his side.

— My Lord, surely there is a strange contradiction in what you do now and what you did a moment ago. Then you called yourself a happy man – and now you weep.

— I was thinking, Xerxes replied — and it came into my mind how pitifully short human life is – for of all these thousands of men not one will be alive in a hundred years' time.

Harry Chapman, in that same white cotton shirt, those same white cotton trousers, was reading the *Histories* of Herodotus in London's Hyde Park in the summer of 1955. His young heart galloped as he followed Xerxes' progress from Sardis (page 432) to Lydia, and thence, passing Mount Ida, entered Trojan territory (page 433), where he reviewed his forces. Reviewing them, he wept (page 433, again), and the eighteen-year-old reader was tempted to weep with him as he lifted his eyes from the glorious book and saw the numerous sunbathers basking in the unexpected heat. How many of them, he wondered, were concerned with the shortness of their earthly existence? It occurred to him that one or two, perhaps, had fatal diseases and were sunning themselves in sheer defiance of the inevitable – making hay, so to speak. These brave souls were indistinguishable from the boys and girls exposing their winter-white skin to the sun's warming rays. He returned to Herodotus, but soon he was sleepy. He took off his shirt and made a pillow of it. He awoke in the early evening with a great thirst, which he quenched in a pub near Marble Arch. He drank lager and lime, a mixture that was very popular with youngsters like him.

— Harry?

— Who is it?

— Only your oldest friend.

— Pamela?

— Yes, you sly elderly sod.

— Am I imagining you? Are you real?

— No, you aren't, and yes, I am.

— I didn't want anyone to know I was here.

— I rang your home, I rang your mobile, and then I rang the police, and after that I rang this hospital. I talked to Sister Nancy Driver, who said you were in the Zoffany Ward.

— Is that where I am? The Zoffany Ward? A second-rate portraitist who lived in a grand house in Chiswick.

— Yes, my dear old duck, that's where you are.

Pamela kissed his forehead and sat down at his bedside.

— Where's Graham, Harry?

— Lost in the jungle somewhere in Sri Lanka.

— Am I your first visitor then?

— Apart from a Catholic priest and a few heroes and villains from literature, yes. I presume Sister Nancy has told you what's the matter with me.

— Yes. As much as she knows.

— Cheer me up, Pam. Are you working?

— Yes, darling, I am. I am essaying the role of the final victim of a serial killer who rapes, strangles and otherwise disembowels ladies *d'un certain âge*. The piece is called – would you believe? – *Fire in the Groin*.

— The fiery groin belongs to the rapist-stroke-killer, *n'est-ce pas?*

— *Mais oui, mon cher*. This will amuse you, Harry. The script requires the actor who plays Colin, he of the blazing genitals, to be quite spectacularly underdeveloped downstairs. It's taken the director several months to find someone courageous enough to waggle his tiny tackle in front of the cameras. It transpires that his grandmother laughed when she saw young Colin's penis and her mockery turned him into a murderer.

— Does he show you the offending weapon, and do you laugh?

— He does, and I don't. So I'm not his final victim, after all. He spares me. I leave the room and call the criminal psychiatrist who has been on Colin's trail and the wretch is found guilty and carted off to prison. *Fire in the Groin* will be transmitted at ten in the evening, when it is assumed that the nation's kiddies will be tucked up in bed dreaming the sweet dreams of the blissfully innocent. Heigh-ho!

— Do you have many lines to learn?

— A few, most of them risible. To think that I was trained to act in Shakespeare, Ibsen and Chekhov – not to mention Greek tragedy – and here I am in my dotage looking at a distraught assassin's apology for a willy with sympathetic understanding. Beggars belief, doesn't it?

— I'm too cynical to be surprised any more.

Much as he loved Pamela, Harry Chapman wished she would leave him. He wanted to be with her in normal, healthy circumstances, not in this dismal place, this anteroom of nowhere.

— You seem very tired, he heard her say, with relief.

— I am.

— I'll be off then, to perfect my performance. Have you the strength to read today's paper?

— I think I have.

— It contains the usual stuff – suicide bombings, starving millions in Africa, Aids on the increase. Just the kind of news to put a smile on your lovely old face.

They kissed goodbye, awkwardly, Continental fashion, and Harry Chapman had cause to wonder if this was to be their very last shared moment. She blew him another kiss as she left what he now knew to be the Zoffany Ward. He closed his eyes and slept.

On waking, the first thing he noticed was the crumpled newspaper Pamela had left behind for him.

— I need reading glasses, he said to Sister, or Nurse, Veronica, who was passing by.

— Why's that?

— I'm blind to words in the evening. It is evening, isn't it?

— Yes, Mr Chapman. It is.

— I want to read this paper my dear friend left for me.

— I'll see what we have in the treasure trove.

The 'treasure trove'? What the hell was she talking about? She had disappeared before he could ask for an explanation.

— I think these will do the trick, she said on her return. Veronica handed him a pair of glasses framed in tortoiseshell.

— From the 'treasure trove'?

— Exactly.

— And what is that, Veronica?

— It's odds and ends. Recent acquisitions from our patients. Neither they nor their relatives have bothered to reclaim them yet. There are spectacles and a couple of rings and a gold necklace and one of those old-fashioned watches men used to carry in their top pocket.

The kind, he did not say, his father depended upon when he was running late on long-ago Sundays.

— Try them on, Mr Chapman.

— Pass me the paper, would you, Veronica?

She did so, and to his sudden, immeasurable delight he found the print positively leaping out at him.

— Oh my, oh my, he heard himself exclaim.

— Enjoy your reading.

— I shall.

It had been his habit, for at least a decade, to turn to the obituary pages first. He needed to know who was in and who was out. Those who were out today were a siren of silent movies — a dipsomaniac with a vampiric sexual appetite — whose struggle with booze and gigolos kept her alive for 106 years, and a Spitfire pilot from the Second World War who had been captured by the Japanese and forced to endure indignities, both physical and mental, that his cheerful equilibrium prevented him from revealing to his wife and children. And then, and there, was a name he recognised, alongside a blurred snapshot of a bald man in what could just be discerned as a velvet suit.

— No, Leo, no.

Yes, it was Leo Duggan, the dapper Leo, his first of many Jewish friends. Leo had died in Holland, his wife of twenty-seven years beside him, the willing party to an assisted suicide. The obituarist recorded that Leo contracted motor neurone disease in his early sixties and had steadily wasted away. It was a skeletal figure, a shadow of the once substantial Leo who took his last flight to Amsterdam. Leo's long career in classical music was celebrated, in particular his generosity towards young composers. Eleanor Duggan, Harry read, faced the possibility of being charged with murder.

He would write her a letter of condolence and support as soon as he was free again.

— What are you doing this Sunday, Harry?

— Nothing special.

— My ma and pa (Leo, uniquely, called his parents Ma and Pa, whereas the other boys at school referred to Mum and Dad) would like my best friend to join us for lunch.

— Thanks, Leo.

— Pa says he'll pick you up at noon. I'll give him your address.

Leo and his parents lived in a district named Golders Green, which Harry Chapman had never visited in any of his long walks around London.

— Golders Green, eh? Little Israel, you mean, remarked his mother. — His family won't be short of a penny or two, if that's where he lives.

Leo's father's car drew up outside the Chapman residence shortly before twelve. Harry couldn't remember what make it was, but it was the grandest motor the street had ever seen. It was a gleaming dark blue.

— Allow me to introduce myself, Mrs Chapman. I am Bernard Duggan, Leo's father.

— I'm pleased to meet you.

— The pleasure's mutual.

— I hope my son behaves himself and watches his table manners.

— I'm sure he will. I've no worries on that score. You must be very proud of him. Such a fine actor at such a young age.

Alice Chapman smiled and nodded by way of reply. She watched as Bernard Duggan drove off with her son beside him on the front seat. She waved as the car glided smoothly along and turned right at the corner.

— Charming woman, your mother, Harry.

— Yes.

— I believe you have a sister.

— She's called Jessie, Mr Duggan.

— Is she as clever as you?

— To be honest, no.

Ashamed at this response, he added:

— But then, she doesn't pretend to be.

He was fifteen, soon to be sixteen, now, and Jack, the ship-boy, had entered the world of his imagination. Jack hadn't alerted Harry to the moral trap he had fallen in – the trap of pride, of arrogance.

— I didn't intend to sound arrogant, Mr Duggan.

— Don't worry. You were speaking the truth. Leo tells me you love music as much as he does.

— I do.

— In that case, I have a wonderful surprise for you. I am not exaggerating. I think you will be impressed. Let's wait and see.

Harry waited, and saw, and heard, and marvelled, after previously marvelling at the palatial house the Duggans occupied – room upon spacious room, with ceilings as high

up, he fancied, as the sky. He thought of his own poky home
and was sick with envy.

— Your eyes are out on stalks, said Leo's mother, Sarah.

— This place is fabulous, Mrs Duggan. It's enormous. I
could easily get lost in it.

— You sweet boy. We're privileged, that's all. Leo assures
me you are rich where it really matters. In your soul, Harry.

Then, to his consternation, the red-headed Sarah Duggan
kissed him.

— Stay rich in spirit, Harry Chapman dear. Regardless.

That word 'regardless', what did she mean by it?
Regardless of any dire human circumstance – was that, in
1952, what she was implying?

— Come and eat. Boys, in my experience, are always
hungry.

Harry Chapman was accustomed to eating his meals
at the wobbly table in the tiny kitchen where his mother
slaved – her expression – at the gas cooker. On special
occasions, such as Christmas, the front-room door was
unlocked, and lunch or dinner was served at the dining
table bequeathed to Alice Bartrip by one of her aristocratic
employers. That circular table was in Harry's possession
still, with a memento of Christopher's worst drunken rage
running across it. He had scarred the wood with a freshly
sharpened carving knife, saying as he did so:

— This is meant for you, Harry Chapman, you piece of
shit.

Twenty years of polishing with beeswax had made the
mark less obvious, more integrated with the stains and
smears bestowed upon it for nearly two centuries.

In 1952, on that memorable afternoon, Harry Chapman
was ushered into a dining room that was wider and longer
than any room he had ever seen, other than those in the

National Gallery and the British Museum. The vast oak table, at which twenty people, he calculated, could eat in comfort, was set for four. He was told where to sit by Mrs Duggan, who remarked that he had pride of place today.

— Thank you.

The first course was on the plate in front of him. He had no idea what it was. Did he have to use a knife and fork? A spoon?

He waited to see which piece of cutlery the Duggans would pick up.

— Do start, Harry. Don't stand on ceremony.

He was terrified now, and ashamed of his ignorance. Then Leo took hold of a spoon, and he did likewise.

— I hope you are fond of avocado pear, Harry.

— I've never had one, Mrs Duggan.

— Well, there's a first time for everything. The secret is to scoop out the flesh. That's a mild vinaigrette on top.

He was slightly more familiar with the second dish, which was chicken, not roasted à la Alice Chapman, but flavoured with an unrecognisable herb.

— It's tarragon, Harry, Leo said.

— We grow it in the garden, along with mint and thyme and rosemary.

— This is delicious, Mrs Duggan.

Chicken was a rare luxury in the Chapman household. His father had a seasonal joke, which he cracked at Easter, at Christmas, at a birthday celebration:

— Not chicken again, woman.

The object of his gentle taunt invariably responded with a fit of pique:

— You haven't had it for six months. I've a good mind to throw it in the dustbin.

— Daddy was joking, Jessie intervened. — He was poking fun at you.

— Was he now? He's got no right to.

The lunch at the Duggans' ended with vanilla ice cream topped with chocolate sauce. He was offered coffee and *petits fours*.

— Are you ready for your surprise, Harry? Bernard Duggan asked as he lit a cigar.

— Yes, please.

— Follow me. Leo, help Sarah to clear the dishes.

— Let me help too.

— Definitely not, Harry. You're our honoured guest.

Leo's father led Harry Chapman along a tiled passage into another vast room, behind which was a conservatory with strange tropical plants in terracotta pots.

— Can you see the surprise? Take a look around.

He looked. He saw comfortable armchairs, a sofa, occasional tables, a vase of chrysanthemums, a fireplace filled with logs.

— Come on, Harry, Bernard Duggan urged.

— It's *that*, isn't it?

He pointed at a glistening object he couldn't give a name to.

— That is a radiogram. A radiogram is a radio and a gramophone combined. I had it sent over from New York.

Leo and his mother joined them.

— Harry is lost for words, Leo.

— That makes a change.

— Shall we put on a long-playing record?

— Yes, Pa.

— Do you like Beethoven, Harry?

— I worship him.

— How does the Seventh Symphony appeal to the worshipper?

— Very much.

— Let's hear it then.

Oh, the bliss of listening to a gramophone record that didn't have to be turned over or changed every few minutes. Arturo Toscanini was the conductor, Harry Chapman recalled, and the performance by the New York Philharmonic was by turns sombre, majestic and dynamically exciting. Once or twice he swore that he heard Toscanini singing along faintly with the divine music.

They sat in silence when the symphony came to an end. Leo was the first to speak.

— Come and see my room, Harry.

— Is it tidy, Leo?

— It could be tidier, Ma.

— Tell me something I don't know.

Leo's room was not the one in which he slept, but a study adjacent to it. Harry's admiring and envious gaze took in all manner of marvellous things – a music stand, with the open score of a sonata for violin and piano by Brahms perched on top; reproductions of paintings by Van Gogh and Gauguin; an imposing desk, complete with reading lamp; the scores of symphonies, concertos and operas, and what seemed to be hundreds of books in French and English.

On the desk, to the right of the lamp, was a framed photograph of a dark-haired woman with lustrous eyes.

— She's beautiful, Leo. Who is she?

— My Aunt Elsa. She was Pa's elder sister.

— Was?

— Was. She died in Auschwitz. That was a German concentration camp in Poland, in case you didn't know.

Innocent, ignorant Harry Chapman knew next to nothing then of Auschwitz, or Belsen, or Dachau or Treblinka or any of the other man-made hells on earth.

— She was gassed. I saw her for the first and last time when I was just over a year old. So Pa told me.

Harry, embarrassed and moved by the sadness in Leo's voice, stared at the titles on the shelves. Leo was, perhaps, an even more serious reader than his friend, though they had certain favourites in common. Almost by chance, Harry pulled out *Histoire de Babar, le petit éléphant*, opened it, and within minutes was wholly captivated by its pictures and its simple text. He turned the pages with increasing delight, once he had recovered from the shock of Babar the little elephant's mother being killed by a wicked hunter in the third illustration.

— There's another Babar book, Harry, said Leo, handing him *Le Voyage de Babar*. — I've had them since I was five. Take them. They're yours now.

— But, Leo –

— I've outgrown them.

Leo smiled warmly.

— Listen, my pretend-Jew of a pal, it's clear to me that you've had a deprived childhood. You've just taught me a lesson. I thought every bright boy and girl had Babar in their lives when they were small. I was wrong. I am happy to pass him on to you.

Harry grasped Leo's arm and thanked him.

— Have fun with Babar and Céleste, and Arthur and Cornelius, and the kind Old Lady.

Thinking of the gift of Babar now, and the gracious youth who had made it, and of the man whose death, lovingly assisted by the devoted Eleanor, he had read about minutes past, Harry Chapman had no alternative but to weep.

He removed the glasses with his free hand. They were a hindrance in his current state.

*   *   *

He was back with the gasworks and the candle factory and Alice Chapman.

— I was hoping they'd adopted you and I'd seen the last of Harry Chapman for ever.

— You're out of luck, Mama.

— I can hear that nasty tone in your voice.

Could she? Could she not recognise it as her own?

— 'Mama'. 'Mama'? How high and mighty have you become?

— It was a joke, like Dad complaining about the frequency of roast chicken for dinner.

— Anyway, enough of that. What's their house like?

— Mr and Mrs Duggan's?

— No, Adam and bloody Eve's. Who else do you think I mean?

— It's more of a mansion than a house. It's huge. Leo has his own rooms. He doesn't have to study at the front-room table the way I have to.

— Ever so sorry, Your Highness, I'm sure. Go on. Tell me about their furniture.

Harry Chapman described the Duggan family's possessions in as much detail as he could muster. It was only when he mentioned the chandelier above the dining table that his mother responded.

— A chandelier, did you say?

— Yes.

— Crystal?

— I suppose so.

He could not remember, waking now, what more she said on the subject of Bernard and Sarah Duggan's chandelier that evening.

Sister Nancy came to feel his pulse and check his blood pressure.

— You were chattering away nineteen to the dozen, Harry. Something about a chandelier.

— Was I really? What's the time?

— Five minutes to midnight. That's another day nearly done with.

It occurred to him suddenly that he had never mentioned the tragic fate of Leo's Aunt Elsa to anybody. He had made it his solemn duty to respect what Leo had told him in earnest.

The face in the photograph appeared to Harry Chapman for a precious instant, and then there was Leo, fifteen again, and then Nancy Driver was tucking him in and praising his courage.

Wednesday

IT WAS THE seventeenth-century divine, Jeremy Taylor, who described a hospital as a 'map of the whole world', and to judge by the raised voices assailing Harry Chapman's ears this morning, Taylor was right. What languages were these? Not Latinate ones, that was certain.

— Who are those people screaming?

— Don't concern yourself, Mr Chapman.

— I want you to tell me who they are.

— It appears we inherited a difficult patient in the middle of the night, Veronica told him. — And now her daughters are here and won't be removed. They don't speak much English. Poor Maciek is trying to reason with them in Polish. We've sent out for an interpreter.

— Where are they from?

— Somalia.

— And what's wrong with the difficult lady?

— I can't answer that. It's a private matter. You must understand.

— Yes.

The noise increased to an ear-shattering level.

— God Almighty, he said. — If the difficult woman is sick, does she need that racket to contend with?

— Good morning, Harry, said Marybeth Myslawchuk.

— I have news for you, Veronica. The interpreter has arrived, and he says they speak two languages in Somalia – Arabic and Somali. He only speaks Arabic, and they only speak Somali. So the farce goes on. We may have to call the police to evict Regan and Goneril.

— You know their names already, Marybeth?

— Marybeth is teasing you, Veronica. Regan and Goneril are the unpleasant daughters of King Lear. That's a play by Shakespeare.

— I can't say I've ever seen it.

He'd seen it first in the 1950s, in an impossibly bad touring production in which the actor playing Lear seldom strayed from the centre of the stage. The supporting cast, with the solitary exception of a passably convincing Fool, had been chosen for their incompetence, the better for the leading man to shine. And shine he did, beneath a spotlight that followed him everywhere. Young as he was, Harry Chapman understood that he was witnessing a travesty, an exercise in vaingloriousness that verged on the farcical. The actors wore ill-fitting wigs and costumes held in place with safety pins. Regan and Goneril were coarser than the coarsest Ugly Sisters in the crudest production of *Cinderella*, and Gloucester – the pitiful, blinded Gloucester – swallowed his lines behind the dentures he sucked when he wasn't speaking.

And yet, Harry Chapman remembered, he was moved to tears when the star said, in an anguished whisper, 'O, let me be not mad, not mad, sweet heaven!' There was real pain in the voice, real terror at the prospect of madness. He fancied he could hear that whisper now, beneath the screaming and shrieking of the difficult woman's daughters.

There was a brief silence, a silence so dramatic that it seemed like the lull before a storm, and then the storm duly broke. The women were keening now, wailing, and their cries were wordless.

— The mother's dead, I think.

He saw that he was talking to himself, for Veronica and Marybeth had rushed away. Regan and Goneril, or whatever their names were, continued howling, and other voices were raised. The doctor they called the Professor was insisting on calm, and his determination to 'lower the collective temperature' soon had an effect. The Professor possessed authority, it was clear. You could tell by the steady way he spoke.

Harry Chapman strained to catch what was being said, but he could only make out the odd phrase, such as 'business as usual' from Nancy Driver. That business did not concern him, it appeared, because he was left alone for what he reckoned was far too long a time.

— Son?

— Is that you, Dad?

— You're the only son I fathered.

— You look younger than I recall you.

— You haven't been born, that's why.

— Then you're not my dad yet.

— Not yet. Wait a bit, son-to-be. Wait until 1937, and then give it a few months before you learn to speak. Your first word might be 'Da-da', unless your mother-to-be decides otherwise. But one thing is certain, I will have some part in bringing you into the world.

The fresh-faced man in front of him was clearly Frank Chapman's younger self, but the voice and the sentiments it was expressing belonged to someone more sophisticated than the father of the Sunday walks.

— Da-da, he said, and laughed. — I am a Dadaist.

— Harry?

The reliable, redoubtable Nancy Driver was at his side.

— It's so quiet, Nancy. Where are the wailing women?

— Gone for good, I hope. I pity the other mourners at their mother's funeral.

— She died?

— While they were here, screaming their heads off. She'd had two strokes before she was brought in and a massive heart attack when they were in full throttle. It was all very distressing, Harry. God rest her soul.

— Amen to that, he almost said.

— Dr Pereira will be seeing you later this morning. Can we expect a poem after he's finished with you?

— I think that could be arranged. I have something life-enhancing in mind.

— I'm pleased to hear it. We need some good cheer to compensate for what we've been through this morning.

'Good cheer'? He hadn't heard the phrase in an eternity: 'Be of good cheer' was in the books and plays he read in childhood.

— If good cheer is what you want, I'll do my best to provide it.

— You're a sweet man, Harry.

He would take issue with that judgement, if he had the energy. How could she know, and declare unequivocally, that he was sweet?

— I wish I were.

— You're sweet while you're in here, and that's all that concerns me and my staff. So many of our patients are unsweet, if I may coin a word.

— I understand.

It remained a mystery to Harry Chapman, after a life-time of writing about the curious ways of human beings, why certain people – few, in his experience – were pleasantly and gently disposed towards their fellow creatures. They seemed not to suffer from the usual sins of pride, envy, avarice and sloth as they carried out their daily tasks. Leo was one such, a kindly intellectual, and so was Aunt Rose, who was barely educated. There were others he'd encountered who had shamed him with their selflessness.

— Rosy Glow's got a dirty secret or two, if you ask me.

— I'm not asking you, Mother. I wouldn't dream of doing that.

— She's craftier than she looks.

— She looks fine to me.

— She's no Virgin Mary –

— If I ask you, which I won't. Do shut up.

— I suppose you think it's clever, speaking to your mother as if she was muck on your shoe.

— Shut up. In the name of all that's decent, shut up.

Marybeth Myslawchuk wondered who it was he was telling to shut up in such an unhappy-sounding voice.

— Oh, someone from my past, Marybeth.

— Someone unpleasant?

— Sometimes.

— Dr Pereira's on his way to you. Veronica and I will make your bed spick and span.

Which they did, with their customary brisk efficiency. Veronica helped him out of his gown and into a fresh replacement, which smelled of bleach.

— *Eau d'hôpital*, he said. — The latest in perfumes.

— I've inhaled worse.

— I'm sure you have, Veronica.

The stench of humanity, Harry Chapman thought. That's what she's referring to. Perhaps, in the last three or four days – he was now unsure how many days had passed – he had made his own contribution to the general malodorousness. A resonant, rancid fart had awoken him in the middle of the night – a terrible harbinger of whatever was to be located in his stomach.

— Good morning, Harry. Or should I say 'afternoon', as it's past twelve o'clock?

— Good afternoon, then, Dr Pereira.

— I have spoken to my colleagues and the three of us have decided to operate tomorrow. We want to remove the lump we have detected near your pancreas. You seem fit enough for such an operation, in our considered opinion.

— What time tomorrow?

— Whenever a theatre becomes available. That's our constant problem. We'll do our best for you.

The fruitseller smiled at Harry Chapman.

— Our very best.

— I'm sure you will, Dr Pereira.

Once the cherubic physician had left, Marybeth Myslawchuk and Nancy Driver reappeared. They were joined, seconds later, by Philip Warren.

— It's poetry time, Harry. You promised us something life-enhancing and cheerful.

— I do believe I did.

— We're waiting, said Nancy, breaking the silence.

— This is an English poem, even though it's an adaptation from the Latin of Ovid, the great Roman poet. It's by Christopher Marlowe, better known as a dramatist. You've heard of *Doctor Faustus*?

— Sure, honey. I saw it when I was a kid at Stratford, Ontario. I found it spooky.

— That's how you're meant to find it. But this isn't spooky at all. Its title is 'Corinnae Concubitus' or 'Going to Bed with Corinna'. Are you ready?

— Yes, the trio chorused.
He began.

> — *In summer's heat, and mid-time of the day,*
> *To rest my limbs upon a bed I lay;*
> *One window shut, the other open stood,*
> *Which gave such light as twinkles in a wood,*
> *Like twilight glimpse at setting of the sun,*
> *Or night being past, and yet not day begun.*
> *Such light to shamefast maidens must be shown*
> *Where they may sport, and seem to be unknown.*
> *Then came Corinna in a long loose gown,*
> *Her white neck hid with tresses hanging down,*
> *Resembling fair Semiramis going to bed,*
> *Or Laïs of a thousand wooers sped.*

Harry Chapman paused momentarily, took a deep breath,
and continued.

> — *I snatched her gown; being thin, the harm was small;*
> *Yet strived she to be covered therewithal;*
> *And striving thus as one who would be cast,*
> *Betrayed herself, and yielded at the last.*
> *Stark naked as she stood before mine eye,*
> *Not one wen in her body could I spy.*
> *What arms and shoulders did I touch and see,*
> *How apt her breasts were to be pressed by me!*
> *How smooth a belly under her waist saw I,*
> *How large a leg, and what a lusty thigh!*
> *To leave the rest, as liked me passing well,*
> *I clinged her naked body, down she fell;*
> *Judge you the rest: being tired she bade me kiss.*
> *Jove send me more such afternoons as this.*

Whatever he was suffering from, it wasn't lapse of memory. He had given a bravura performance, imagining himself in a more congenial bed with a Corinna whose 'large leg' and 'lusty thigh' were those of a Corin.

— We enjoyed that. A bit risqué, isn't it?

— Who's the Semi— what's his name?

— Semiramis. She was the founder of Babylon, Nancy, and the wife of Ninus, King of Assyria. She ruled over the country after his death. And as for Laïs, she was a Corinthian concubine who really did have thousands of lovers. In her old age, when her looks had gone, she took to the bottle and died an alcoholic.

— I'm learning something new every day you're here.

He was warmed by her remark, warmed because of the teacher in him, the man who was most content when he was passing on arcane information, the best information there is, in his peculiar view.

He felt depleted now. He had spent himself, reciting the poem. He wanted only to drift away, courtesy of Dr Pereira. Maciek Nazwisko's 'best sleep' was an alluring prospect.

It was not to be. It was definitely not to be while there was bustle in the ward. Nancy Driver had offered to instal a television set a couple of days earlier but he had declined her offer.

— It would distract you, Harry. Take your mind off things.

— I'm happy as I am, he'd lied.

— You always have the radio.

— Yes. I might listen to some music later on.

But he hadn't, and he wondered why. It was unlike him to pass an entire day without Bach or Schubert – especially Schubert – to afford the emotional and intellectual stimuli he had craved from childhood. Yet the headphones within his reach remained unused. It was as if he had no need to have his savage breast calmed and soothed.

— I would prefer not to listen. That is my preference.

— Bartleby?

— I have answered to that name on occasion.

— Not today?

— Today I would prefer not to.

Ah, that phrase, that metaphysical decision to neither do nor say anything practical, anything that exerted the body or mind, was as the loveliest solemn music to Harry Chapman's ears. Bartleby's preferred pronouncements were like plainsong.

There he stood, the shadowy scrivener, in what looked like a nightgown.

— Are you a patient here?

— I am beyond being cared for.

— I wish I were.

— You do not wish any such thing. You would prefer to live. You would prefer not to die.

It was true, and he was gratified to hear it from such a sepulchral source, who stood there no longer.

— You're right, Bartleby. I wish to go on living.

If only, Harry Chapman thought, to read about you again, to enjoy your cheerless company. He had come to Herman Melville's 'Bartleby' late in life, when he was forty, in the Midwestern wastes of North America, and the skeletal clerk had been by his side ever since. He was still unsure, careful reader that he was, what the short, beautiful novel really meant. It refused to be summed up neatly, to be encapsulated in a paragraph or so, for Bartleby lived on beyond the confines of a closed book. He had faded away into death, but he was nevertheless immortal.

*   *   *

Shortly after waking, Harry Chapman realised that he'd been granted Maciek Nazwisko's 'best sleep'. And then he wondered if he had simply dozed off for a few minutes.

— The weather today is simply glorious, he heard a woman trumpeting from somewhere down the ward. — There's lovely misty sunshine and the leaves that are still on the trees are either golden or red. That heavenly russet colour. You must get better, Maurice, before autumn turns to winter.

If Maurice, whoever Maurice was, made a reply, Harry Chapman didn't hear it.

— I was thinking to myself as I was driving along how Maurice would appreciate those divine autumnal hues. Who was it described autumn as a 'season of mists and mellow fruitfulness'?

In case Maurice didn't know, or was too ill to answer, Harry Chapman shouted:

— Keats. It was John Keats.

The trumpeter did not respond. Perhaps he had embarrassed her.

— Oh, I remember, she continued after a long pause. — Am I right in thinking it was Keats?

Tell her she's right, Maurice, he refrained from saying. Tell her she is spot on.

— Keats was how old when he went over to the other side, Maurice? Twenty-five at the most. And here you are, you rogue, at seventy plus. You've been a very lucky boy.

Harry Chapman was intrigued now. Who was this woman and what did she have to do with Maurice?

— Very lucky, and very, very naughty, she went on, with a hint of sauciness in her braying voice. — Oh, Maurice, you have been wicked beyond the call of duty.

What had Maurice done to be deemed 'wicked' in such

a complimentary manner? And how far 'beyond the call of duty' had he sinned?

Oh, here was a story to be told, to be relished.

— That trip to Morocco in '89. She chuckled. — That was a trip and a half. What you got up to in Tangier would have brought a blush to Casanova's cheeks, you dirty reprobate. Isn't that the utter truth?

Yet again, there was no sound from Maurice.

— So you don't deny it? You'd be a copper-bottomed hypocrite if you did. What have I just said, Maurice? 'Copper-bottomed'. There were plenty of copper bottoms in Morocco, weren't there? Some more coppery than others, if your disgusting tales are to be believed.

Harry Chapman hoped the woman would feel inspired to repeat at least one of Maurice's disgusting tales.

— Here's hoping, he whispered.

— I wouldn't begin to soil my lips by reminding you of the things you told me.

The killjoy, he thought. The pestilential killjoy.

— I bet you made most of them up, just to shock me. Those positions, she exclaimed with a vocal shudder. — Those *impossible* positions. Even an Olympic medallist would have baulked before attempting them.

Harry Chapman was at his most attentive. He had always prided himself on his ability to listen, that rarest of gifts. He waited, and then waited, for further revelations. He was becoming impatient when he heard:

— Maurice, my old darling, you must set your house in order. You really, really must. Think of poor Fritz, and of Mona, and those weird, weird twins, Boris and Jocelyn. Don't you feel a smidgen of guilt regarding them?

Maurice's guilt, as far as Harry Chapman could ascertain, was unexpressed.

— Well, that's a relief of sorts, that you acknowledge, in your curmudgeonly way, the pain you put them through.

There was another, deeper silence, in which Harry Chapman pondered the fates of poor Fritz, and of Mona, and those weird, weird twins, Boris and Jocelyn. Who were they, and what in God's name had Maurice done to them?

— It's Boris I feel for most. You put him through hell, if in the nicest fashion. The nicest fashion you knew. It was the nearest you ever came to nicest.

She was not speaking vindictively. Her trumpet had not been muted, yet it contained no trace of hatred.

— Maurice, did you ever love me?

Maurice was tongue-tied, as usual.

— Of course you did. Silly question. I know you did. The children we had together are living proof you did. That's the only proof I have.

Harry Chapman was beginning to pity the jocular brayer. He sensed sorrow on the horizon.

— But there it is, and there we are, and what's done is done.

The unknown woman, the present or past wife or lover of the wicked Maurice – he of the impossible positions – had fallen into what Harry Chapman supposed was a sorrowful silence. He came to this judgement after several minutes. He felt deprived of essential information. For example: what was the precise nature of the weirdness credited to the weird, weird twins Boris and Jocelyn? Was Jocelyn a man or a woman? Jocelyn was one of those names – along with Hilary and Evelyn – that was defiantly sexless.

The silence, sorrowful or otherwise, persisted, and Harry Chapman forgot about Maurice and Morocco and Fritz and Mona and the weird, weird twins. Night had descended and all he could see in the dim glow was the nurse on duty sitting at the reception desk reading a book by – yes – Harry Chapman. She raised her head at one point and he recognised Nurse Mullen, who had offended him – how many days ago was it? – with her philistine observation that poetry had to be spouted rather than spoken.

She rose from her seat and came over to his bedside.

— There's a visitor for you, Mr Chapman. She's walked all the way to the hospital from your house. I do declare she's pining for you.

— She? Who is she?

— I know this isn't regular, Mr Chapman, but we're making an exception for you. It's your cat.

— Puss?

— Is that what you call her?

— Yes. When I was with Christopher, we gave our cats fancy names. There was Omar Khayyám, a monstrous Persian; Orpheus, a tabby who listened to music; and Jezebel, a black-and-white minx. But Graham and I know this one as Puss, pure and simple.

— Puss, Puss, come to your master, commanded Nurse Mullen, and the dumpy tortoiseshell obligingly padded into view. She hesitated a moment, her green eyes sparkling, and then she leapt in the air and landed on his bed. She purred – and cats only purr when they are happy – and licked his face. He stroked her back and pulled her tail gently and ran a finger through the white patch under her chin. She purred even louder in response.

— I'll leave you two lovers alone, Mr Chapman. She's got twenty minutes and that's her absolute limit.

Puss spread herself across his chest, adjusting her body to achieve maximum comfort. He stroked her again, and the thick fur crackled with electricity. He felt her rough tongue on his hand.

What was this? Could it be that there was another cat in the ward? As far as he knew, Puss had no feline friends or even casual acquaintances, yet he could detect the distant tormented serenading of a tom whose lust needs to be satiated. The maddened creature was moving nearer and nearer, his yowls increasing in volume, while Puss slept contentedly.

This was a spectral cat before him, a very ghost, a creeping, yowling skeleton. Harry Chapman knew on the instant that he was Jeoffrey, the comforter of the poet Christopher Smart, keeping the 'Lord's watch in the night against the adversary'.

— Go to your master, Jeoffrey, he whispered, in order not to disturb or waken Puss.

A small, plump, dirtily dressed man of forty-one was now praying sonorously in – in – where was it?

— St James's Park, answered the man. — *For I blessed God in St James's Park till I routed all the company.*

Yes, it was poor Kit Smart, as the London dandies and wits of the 1750s dubbed him, removing his filthy, soiled linen as the rain fell, sending the rabble who had mocked the madman scuttling for cover. He was soon as bare as Adam in Eden.

— *For to worship naked in the Rain is the bravest thing for the refreshing and purifying the body.*

— Her time's up, announced Nurse Mullen. — She's been with you twenty-two minutes already. Sister Driver will have my guts for garters if she ever finds out I allowed a cat to visit you.

— Thank you, Nurse Mullen, he said, as she lifted Puss from him and cradled her in her arms.

Jeoffrey's ghost remained, washing his bony back with a vanished tongue and the bones that were once his forepaws. His master, clothed again, beamed down on him.

— He is the cleanest of the quadrupeds. And the Good Samaritan is not yet come.

— I've met him. He exists. Or rather, she does.

So Harry Chapman told the by turns radiant and disconsolate Christopher Smart, former occupant of the madhouse at St Luke's Hospital and latterly resident in Bedlam, that once, long ago, in his own deranged younger days, he had been rescued from a watery grave by a Good Samaritan named Eileen. It was very early on a winter's morning when she saw him poised to leap from a parapet into the swirling Thames. She had advised him to wait a minute before making such a final decision and the calmness with which she proffered the suggestion caused him to turn and look at her. She had smiled. She had wondered, calmly, if his life was as bad as he believed or imagined. He'd replied that it was worse than bad, and she'd invited him to tell her how and why. He'd hesitated – of course, he'd wavered, and doubted, and paused – before he accepted her invitation by jumping down to the pavement.

The stranger, who now identified herself as Eileen Robb, said there was a café nearby that stayed open throughout the night. It specialised in extra strong tea and sandwiches of the kind known as doorsteps. Nothing fancy; nothing cordon bleu. But it was warm, and the husband and wife who ran the place were friendly.

The tea was indeed strong and the bacon sandwich mountainous. Eileen Robb watched him as he widened his mouth to its limits in order to eat. Between bites, he told her about his failed career as an actor, of the sense of inadequacy that afflicted him whenever he attempted to write. She listened and occasionally nodded. When he'd finished, she remarked that, as far as she could judge, his life wasn't that bad, and far too precious, in her opinion, to sacrifice. Was he ill, she asked him, with an incurable disease? He had to answer no. Her advice to Harry, for such she knew him to be, was to persevere, to carry on, to regard every mistake and drawback as the bottom rungs on the ladder to success. Failure was often necessary to a person's development. And besides, she reminded him, he was young, and the wide world was his to discover.

They parted at around four o'clock, the dawn still some hours away. She walked with him to a bus stop and waited with him until the bus arrived. He waved to her from his seat on the upper deck, and she waved back. On the way home, it occurred to him that he'd asked her no questions about herself, and he felt ashamed. He never saw Eileen Robb, his very good Samaritan, again. He hoped, as the years went by, that she would contact him. He was at his most hopeful when his first book was published. She would write to him, surely, he reasoned. But the letter he wanted to receive, signed Eileen Robb, did not reach him.

He stopped talking. Poor Kit Smart and his spectral Jeoffrey had gone. He hadn't seen them leave.

— Just checking your blood pressure, Harry, said Marybeth Myslawchuk. — And your pulse.

— Thank you.

— No need to thank me. It's my job, honey.

— Tell me something.

— I might if you could be more precise.

— There was a woman here earlier today visiting a man called Maurice.

— What do you want to know?

— Who she is. Who he is. Idle curiosity.

— I had the afternoon off, but I'll try and find out for you. Maurice has been moved to another ward, that much I can reveal. He's in a fragile state.

— I'm not surprised.

— Why is that, Harry? Are you cleverer than the doctors?

— I was being facetious. Maurice's wife, or ex-wife, or lover has a bedside manner beyond compare. She brayed at the wretched Maurice from start to finish. I could almost picture him wilting under the onslaught.

— I'll do some detective work on your behalf. If the information will make you a happier man.

— I doubt that it will. But it might just divert me for an hour or so.

Imagine a great green forest somewhere in Africa. Picture an elephant who has just been born. His doting mother gives him the name Babar. He is her first child and she loves him very much. She places him in a hammock strung between two palm trees and rocks him to sleep with her trunk, singing softly to him all the while.

Babar grows bigger, as elephants and humans do. He plays with the other little elephants, some of whom have friendly monkeys perched on their bodies. One day, when Babar is riding happily on his mother's back, a wicked hunter, who has hidden himself behind a bush, shoots at them, killing Babar's mother.

A monkey, who has been watching, scampers off and all the birds in the air disappear into the blue. The hunter – is he the wicked Maurice, whose impossibly positioned misadventures in Morocco are the talk of the Zoffany Ward? – runs up to capture the orphaned Babar. But the nimble Babar escapes being captured, and keeps on running for several days, until he comes to a town . . .

— How old are you, Harry Chapman?

— You know my age, Mother, if anyone does.

— How old are you?

— Oh, for God's sake stop pestering me. I'm fifteen.

— If you're fifteen, soon to be sixteen, what are you doing with a book about a baby elephant?

— It's a present from Leo. He read it when he was very small. He said I've had a deprived childhood because there was no Babar to make me smile and be happy.

— Deprived? That's a fine way for a boy to speak whose father is as rich as he is, I must say.

— Must you?

— Yes, I must. What time did we have for baby elephants? Especially French ones. It is in *parlez-vous*, isn't it?

That was his father's expression, that *parlez-vous*. It was virtually all he knew of the language, surrounded as he was in the trenches of Flanders by the English mates whose names he called out on the day of his dying.

— I never could get a handle on *parlez-vous*, he'd confided to his son on a walk back from the park in the long ago. — But you'll be different, you clever little sod.

But here was Babar, out of breath and tired, arriving in the town and seeing hundreds of houses. As well as houses, there are broad streets known as boulevards, and motor cars and buses. He looks with particular interest at two men in conversation on a street corner and marvels at how well dressed they are. He would like some fine clothes, too, but has no idea how to acquire them. Luckily for him, a very rich Old Lady who has a fondness for little elephants understands that he is longing for a smart suit. The Old Lady, who is wearing a long red dress and a fur tippet, takes pity on Babar and hands him her purse . . .

— Whoever heard of an elephant going to a department store and buying a green suit, a derby hat and shoes with spats?

— It's a fantasy, Mother. It's make-believe.

— Make-believe never put bread and butter on the table.

Babar is so pleased with his first clothes, in which he looks very elegant, that he goes to a photographer to have his picture taken. Just imagine: an elephant posing in front of an old-fashioned tripod camera.

This being a book by a Frenchman, when Babar has dinner with his friend the Old Lady, he balances a glass of red wine – a vintage claret, perhaps – on the tip of his trunk. Only a few pages back, he was in the African wilderness, and now here he is, dressed up to the nines, eating soup and ham, and enjoying civilised discourse with a wealthy widow. Harry Chapman, at fifteen, assumed she was a widow, like his mother. Anyway, she lives alone, with only a tiny dog in tow.

Babar moves into the Old Lady's house, and every morning he joins her as she exercises, doing press-ups, and afterwards has a satisfying soak in the bath . . .

— Can you really believe, clever-dick Harry Chapman, that an elephant – an elephant! – could plonk his bum on a seat made for men, women and children? You saw the one at the zoo, when your dad and me took you and Jessie for a treat, and he opened his backside – didn't he? – and it was like a deluge what came out of him.

Deluge? Had she said 'deluge'? Maybe she had. It was in her character to surprise her son occasionally with an unexpected word. The elephant at London Zoo in 1947 had indeed emitted a deluge of mud-coloured shit, which Harry and Jessie witnessed with giggling fascination.

I wouldn't like that keeper's job. He's ready and waiting with his shovel. How many times a day do you think he has to clear up after Jumbo?

— Why don't you go and ask him, Frank, seeing as how you're so interested?

Babar was too refined, too considerate a mammal to have behaved as that huge, ungainly beast behaved six decades past. He would have been discreet in his ablutions, this king-in-waiting, Harry Chapman informed his constantly down-to-earth mother slyly.

— King, did you say?

— I did.

He showed Alice Chapman the illustration of King Babar and Queen Céleste in their bridal-cum-coronation robes, brought from the nearest town by an obliging dromedary, who arrives in the nick of time. The previous king, he explained to her, had died as the result of eating a bad mushroom. He had turned green from top to toe.

— Hoof. Hooves, she corrected him. — Elephants have hooves.

— Yes, Mother. You could be right. But I think they're called feet as well.

— It just so happens I bought a quarter-pound of mushrooms today. I hope there's not a bad one among them. I don't fancy the idea of you and your sister going green.

He saw those mushrooms now, lightly peppered and salted, fried gently in a dab of butter.

Suddenly, as if from nowhere, he caught the sound of a man singing. The voice and the tune and the words were familiar to him. He listened intently as the debonair singer referred to feeling awfully low in a world turned cold. But there was hope. All he had to do was picture his beloved and immediately he felt aglow with love and happiness at the way she would be looking tonight.

This isn't any man, this is Fred Astaire, in white tie and tails, wearing a top hat set at a jaunty angle. His hands are elegantly gloved and he is carrying a cane. He is dressed, as always, for a special occasion.

— Your Majesties, he says, bowing deeply.

— I believe, Mr Astaire, that you wish to dance with my beloved consort, Queen Céleste.

— That is true, Your Majesty. It would be the greatest honour for me to lead Her Majesty on to the floor.

— I, too, should be honoured, says Queen Céleste, in a surprisingly squeaky voice for such a very large lady. — It has long been my dream – if you will forgive me, my dearest husband – to hoof it with the unparalleled Mr Fred Astaire.

King Babar instructs the band (the motliest crew of two monkeys, three ostriches, a leopard, a tiger, a camel, a snake, a zebra and an antelope) to strike up.

— Take it away, he commands.

And there it is again, the blissful song by Jerome Kern, first heard by Harry Chapman coming out of the eccentric wireless in the apology for a kitchen where Alice slaved over a thousand meals.

— He's got a lovely voice, remarked his usually malevolent mother. – And he's not a bad dancer, come to that.

Queen Céleste alights from her throne and offers her front legs to Fred Astaire, who takes them in his outstretched hands. Soon they are in a decorous embrace, and Fred – his cane and top hat discarded – leads her effortlessly in what he tells his glowing partner is a foxtrot. Her ball gown billows in the spring breeze.

— You are very light on your feet, Your Majesty.

— Back hooves, Mr Astaire, she corrects him, sounding for an instant like Alice Chapman.

— I beg your pardon, Your Majesty. May I observe that you have a finer feel for the music, for the rhythm, than has Miss Ginger Rogers?

— You may, responds Céleste, reverting to her regal squeak. — I am flattered. It is the highest compliment I have been paid since my cousin Babar asked for my hand in marriage.

Mr Astaire hears himself singing about the laugh that wrinkles the regal nose and instantly corrects himself:

— I'm so sorry, Your Majesty, *trunk*.

— Apology accepted, Mr Astaire.

— *And that laugh that wrinkles your trunk,* sings Fred, seeming to mean every word as he tells the elephantine queen that his foolish heart is touched by the very sound of her laughter and the sight of her puckering trunk

— That serpent is a remarkable clarinettist, Your Majesty.

— Isn't he? Funny what a fang can do, don't you think? Snakes have not been looked upon favourably since that regrettable business in the Garden of Eden, but Oscar – bless his cobra's chilly cotton socks – is a very loyal courtier in addition to being, as you perceive so cogently, a talented musician.

— He's the equal of Benny Goodman.

— We, King Babar and myself, will convey your appreciation of his playing to him.

— You are most gracious, Your Majesty.

— All in the day's work, Mr Astaire. If a queen cannot be gracious, what is a queen for?

— You speak wisely, ma'am.

— A monarch must have wisdom.

— I wish every monarch had been as wise as you. Then history would have a prettier tale to tell.

The dance comes to a triumphant end. King Babar leads the applause.

— Bravo, brava, the animals cry.

— *Le jour de gloire est arrivé,* shouts the Old Lady, an ardent royalist where elephants are concerned, but otherwise something of a revolutionary, it occurs to Harry Chapman, who — by the sound of it — is alone in the Zoffany Ward.

— Your friend Maurice is back with us. He's sleeping peacefully.

— That's good, Marybeth.

— The woman who came to see him today mothered three of his fourteen children. Her name is Patience.

— Patience? That is wonderful. Is, or was, the impatient Patience his wife?

— He doesn't agree with the institution of marriage. He is an advocate of free love.

— Ah, that would account for the impossible positions.

— What on earth are you talking about, Harry?

He explained to Marybeth what the woman called Patience had trumpeted to the somnolent Maurice. The trip to Morocco in '89, and the things he got up to in Tangier that would have brought a blush to Casanova's cheeks, the plethora of copper bottoms and those *impossible* positions that even an Olympic gold medallist would have lacked the courage to attempt — all this he recounted to the bemused Canadian, whose smile broadened with each revelation.

— My, my. He looks washed out right now. I shall be surprised if he regains the energy to continue on with his former pursuits.

— Does he have a career outside that of a free lover? Or is that his full-time occupation?

— I didn't enquire, Harry. If he's compos mentis in the morning, I'll ask him.

— I'd be obliged. What's the time?

— Late. Eleven thirty. Or twenty-three thirty, if you prefer.

— Tomorrow's my big day, I believe.

— It'll be a doddle, Harry. You're not to worry. Trust me, honey.

Yes, he supposed he trusted her, just as he trusted Nancy Driver. He was in their proverbial good hands.

— Trust them, Harry, advised his Aunt Rose. — They want to make you well again.

— In body, Auntie. I think my soul's beyond repair. What's left of it.

— This is meant for you, Harry Chapman, you selfish piece of shit, Christopher shrieked as he scarred the table bequeathed to Alice Bartrip by a grateful aristocratic employer. — This knife is meant for your heart.

— You're drunk.

— Oh, you and your writer's insight. Of course I'm fucking drunk. You'd make a Mother Superior hit the bottle.

— Go away, Christopher. Go away, he begged the swaying bloated man he had loved for all too brief, and all too long, a time.

Three Christophers had been with him: Christopher Marlowe, stabbed to death in a Deptford tavern; Christopher Smart, shoved in and out of asylums, abandoning his family, calling out to God for salvation; and Christopher Riley, who had declared his love for Harry Chapman with an intense conviction that could not be denied or doubted.

— Have I made my feelings clear?

— You have.

— So you've got the message?

— Yes, I have.

— You won't get a better offer.

Christopher Riley, the seriously lapsed Catholic, had spoken the absolute truth in 1964. Harry Chapman, then, could not foresee ever getting a better offer. He was fated, doomed, to accept it.

The thought of that love, that stifling, suffocating love, from which he was unable to extricate himself, however much he tried to, chilled Harry Chapman, whose only immediate hope of warmth was to be wafted into dreamless sleep.

Thursday – Friday – Saturday

MACIEK NAZWISKO HAD shaved the stubble from Harry Chapman's face and the hairs on his stomach and around his cock and balls. He had performed his duty with considerate expertise.

— Do not move, Mr Chapman. I am trying not to cut you.

And now Veronica was washing him, preparing his body for the ongoing slaughter or investigation or whatever Dr Pereira cared to call it.

— There, there, she murmured, as if to a fearful child.

Was he frightened? His brain wasn't telling him so, but could it be that Veronica was seeing signs of abject terror in his eyes, in the face she was sponging with such delicate attentiveness?

— Where are you from, Veronica?

— You asked me that question the other day and I gave you the answer. Have you forgotten?

— I must have. Mea culpa.

— The answer's still the same, Mr Chapman. My family hails from Odessa, but I was born in Bristol.

— I shan't forget a second time.

— You must have more important matters on your mind.

Yes, indeed. Yes, Veronica, I am thinking of being alive at this moment and, perhaps, not being alive when the medics have finished with me. And if I could tell you, which I don't wish to, that I am not afraid, for reasons far beyond logic, you in your infinite kindness would probably not believe me.

— There, there, she said again. — You're immaculate, Mr Chapman.

— I hope the surgeon is appreciative.

— He will be.

— Good evening, Harry, said Nancy Driver. — I've come to get your autograph. Who is your next of kin?

— Kin? I may have a cousin or two somewhere on the planet, but my nearest and dearest are all dead. I'm a sad old orphan.

— We need a name.

— Graham. Graham Weaver.

— Is he the friend who's in Sri Lanka?

— He is. Have you made contact with him yet?

— We've sent messages. There's been no reply from him in person. What's his London address?

— The same as mine.

She handed him the form, which was attached to a clipboard, and he signed and dated it.

— My final words, perhaps.

— No, Harry. Absolutely not.

— You cheer me, Sister Nancy.

— It shouldn't be very long before we take you down to theatre.

Theatre? The magic word of his adolescence. Harry Chapman, destined to be Hamlet, Richard the Second, Romeo and then Macbeth and Lear. The lights going down in the auditorium, the curtain rising, the two hours' traffic commencing – how exciting he had found it all then, sitting in the gallery, the cheapest, most distant part of the house, with Pamela sometimes beside him. However tragic the events onstage – the stabbings; the poisonings; the slayings; the suicides – they seemed to happen in a world unencumbered with gasworks and candle factories, a world bewitchingly elsewhere.

Today's theatre, which Nancy had assured him he would soon be visiting, was not such a place of enchantment. He would not be a hero this evening, thanks to the anaesthetist, but rather a passive victim, a body on a slab, while the heroics, the big dramatic gestures, would be played out by Dr Pereira and Mr Russell and – perhaps – the mysterious, authoritative Professor. Today he would be almost no one, a purely physical object to be dissected, a Harry Chapman known solely for the lump near his pancreas, a Harry Chapman in name only, on the tag identifying him, not the imaginative, creative Harry Chapman, the Harry Chapman he had willed and made himself to be, outside the common herd who were the constant, prevailing subject of his writings.

'The common herd': that was an expression to be regretted, even if he'd only thought it. There was a special dignity in being a commoner, as he had often made plain.

— You always did believe you were a cut above the rest of us, didn't you?

There was no mistaking that vinegary voice.

— I suppose I did, once upon a long, long time ago, Mother.

— You were a stuck-up little tyke.

Ah, that beautiful word. How lovely to hear it again. 'Tyke': a mongrel child, an imp, and in Australia a Roman Catholic.

— I wasn't a mongrel child, was I?

— You were what you were, she answered, gnomically.

— And that was adorable, Aunt Rose intervened. — You and your sister were adorable children. You were little treasures.

Before his mother could make a predictable riposte, Harry Chapman was suddenly conscious of being lifted from his bed and placed on to a gurney.

— The anaesthetist is ready for you, Harry.

— But am I ready for him, Nancy?

— It's a her, my dear. And very capable she is.

He was pushed along corridors and into a capacious lift, which plunged downwards.

— He doesn't look too good, someone whispered to another.

— It's bad, whatever it is he's got, the another remarked to the someone, who were both beyond his vision.

— You see bad sights, working in here.

That was the someone again, who inspired the another to observe:

— You do indeed. A truer word was never said.

Who were these cheerful souls, these loud whisperers?

— He's as pale as my Alf was, the day he toppled over.

— But he's all right now, isn't he?

— Yes and no. He has to mind what he eats and drinks. He used to be partial to steak and kidney, but his stomach can't abide it any more. He swears he's in purgatory when his nose gets a whiff of it.

— Poor Alf. Still, he's lucky to be with us, steak and kidney notwithstanding.

The someone – or was it the another? – pondered the accuracy of this observation.

The lift doors opened, and Harry Chapman was propelled

along a wide corridor, at the end of which was a room where a woman who introduced herself as Dr Helen Burgess greeted him. She checked his pulse, his blood pressure, and told him she was confident enough to go ahead.

And go ahead she did, and soon Harry Chapman found himself slowly vanishing, and then he had no sense at all that he was anyone . . .

. . . and then a distant music came to his awakening ears. Schubert's tormented winter traveller could be heard far off on the snowy plain. Three blood-red suns suddenly appeared in the sky above the wanderer and then as suddenly evaporated.

The singer – a portly baritone in a tattered frock coat – was moving closer to Harry Chapman. He was singing of the comforting darkness that would be his last consolation. Not far from him, barely visible, was an old organ-grinder playing on his hurdy-gurdy.

> — *Wunderlicher Alter, soll ich mit dir gehn?*
> *Willst zu meinen Liedern deine Leier drehn?*

sang the baritone, and so did the patient in the theatre, in a voice raw with feeling.

— Well done, Sunshine.

The man who was addressing the waking Harry Chapman looked vaguely familiar.

— I'm Mr Russell. I opened you up. You may not have realised it, but you were singing towards the end of the operation. The words sounded like German.

Harry Chapman, unable to speak because of the equipment in his mouth, nodded assent.

— You are in the intensive care unit, in case you don't recognise your surroundings. You will stay here for a day or two.

A bespectacled woman with her hair in a tight bun appeared at the doctor's side.

— This is Nurse Dunckley. She's in charge. She'll be at your beck and call.

— Think of me as Jeanette, my love, said the nurse. I'm a friendly soul, Harry. I may call you 'Harry', mayn't I?

He hadn't heard 'mayn't I?' in ages, if ever. Since he could neither smile nor speak, he managed a cursory nod.

— So we're Jeanette and Harry, my love.

— I'll check up on you later, Sunshine, the doctor promised, and left.

Why, Harry Chapman wanted to know, was Mr Russell calling him 'Sunshine'? He would ask Jeanette for an explanation, as soon as he could form a coherent sentence.

— You're a very handsome Harry, my love. We want you to stay in the world as long as possible.

Oh, that was a reassuring observation from the lanky Jeanette, whose inamorato he had inexplicably become.

— She's flannelling you, snapped the Clytemnestra of the gasworks and the candle factory. She's a cold-hearted bitch behind all that smarmy talk. 'My love', indeed. Watch her carefully, Harry Chapman.

What else was there for him to do – cabined, cribbed and confined as he was in this brightly lit ward?

He longed, now, for the company of Sister Nancy, of Marybeth, of Philip and Maciek, of the dutiful Veronica. They were his new-found friends. He wanted to be back among them, hearing their familiar voices, seeing their concerned or irritated expressions, entertaining them – if that was what he'd been doing – with the poetry he had made his own.

— We'll have you up and about in no time, my love. No time at all.

Had there ever been a golden age in the long life of Harry Chapman? He tried to recall it as he lay – dying, perhaps – in the room reserved for those poised on the very brink. It was a futile question, he soon decided. He'd had, in common with countless others, moments of happiness, of well-being. Moments? No, there were hours, days, weeks even, he could summon up if he applied himself to the task of remembering. One image, and one alone, came to him without effort. He was standing in the courtyard of the Forte Belvedere, looking down on the city of Florence on a May morning, marvelling at the exquisite colours – mostly pink and green – of the Duomo and the Campanile. The day was gradually heating up, but at ten o'clock it was relatively mild. Here was paradise on earth. It was as if his past had been obliterated. Harry Chapman, at the age of thirty-one, was like a slim Cortez, silent upon his very own peak in Darien. He'd smiled at the notion then, and he might have smiled again, had he not been encumbered with tubing.

This young man in uniform would father Harry Chapman twenty years into the future. For now, though, he was somewhere in France, his son supposed.

— You suppose correctly. I'm in the land of parlee-vous. But my pal here has shifted off to heaven already.

— Your pal? Is he dead?

— As much as he'll ever be. The Hun's bullet got him while he was smiling. That's why he looks like he's grinning at the moon. I'm sitting alongside him till someone carts him off and buries him. I think he'll be here with me watching it for the whole night.

— What's his name?

— George. I tell you, boy, if I had pen and paper to hand I'd write letters home to everyone saying how happy I am to be alive. God help me, it takes a pal dying next to you to remind you what a precious thing your life is.

— What day is it, Dad?

— Twenty-third of December, 1917. Christmas will soon be upon us. What a laugh. What a bloody farce.

Then Harry Chapman, ninety years on, saw George's broken-toothed grin, and Frank's living hand clutching George's lifeless one, and then there was nothing but whiteness before his eyes, and then he was conscious of a bespectacled woman assuring him that he was making wonderful progress.

— You're a man and a half, my love.

— Good morning, Sunshine. How was your night?

How was his night? Well, he seemed to recall that the thirty-one-year-old Frank Chapman had appeared to him, a dead private named George at his side. He was unable to mention this to the inquisitive doctor as he was still unable to speak. Why did Mr Russell ask Sunshine how his night had been, knowing as he did that Sunshine could not reply?

— We'll be dismantling some of your scaffolding later today. The catheter will be the first to go.

The catheter? What catheter? He was unaware that he was catheted, if such a verb existed.

— You'll be your old self again soon, Sunshine.

'Sunshine': Harry Chapman approved of his new name. No matter that Mr Russell probably addressed all his patients – men and women – in this determinedly cheerful fashion. For the moment, for a day or so, he was Sunshine.

That afternoon, if afternoon it was, he heard a man saying:

— I had a left leg twenty-four hours ago. Now there's nothing there.

— I know, a woman's voice responded.

— You don't know. You don't know at all. You're standing on two feet, aren't you?

— Yes, darling.

— What bloody future have I got? Playing Long John Silver at children's parties. That's about the limit of my ambitions.

— Don't be silly.

Harry Chapman had read *Treasure Island* again during the summer and had been surprised to rediscover that John Silver was a decorous individual, capable of the most disarming courtesy. He had forgotten that the duplicitous sea-cook had a black wife, who kept a tight rein on his ill-gotten money.

— Eunice, go to a pet shop and buy a parrot for me. We'll call him 'Captain Flint' and teach him to squawk 'Pieces of eight. Pieces of eight.'

— Oh, you darling idiot, Johnny.

— I can't think of a better alternative right now. Can you?

Eunice — whatever the colour of her skin — did not reply to Johnny's question.

— You can't, Eunice. You just fucking can't.

— There's no need for that kind of language.

— Why the fuck not?

— Oh, Johnny, you're not sounding like you.

— It's not every day I lose a leg.

— I know.

— Stop saying you know.

Harry Chapman, so near and yet so far from one-legged Johnny and hapless Eunice, wanted to know about the life they had led together before yesterday.

— You'll leave me now, won't you? You have a wonderful excuse at last.

— That's unkind, Johnny.

— But true.

— No, it isn't. It isn't true at all.

That unlikely marriage-guidance counsellor Harry Chapman wished he could be tubeless and upright, free from his invalid's bed. He had an absurd need to advise the pair behind the screen on how best to accommodate themselves to Johnny's misfortune. As needs go, this one was so absurd as to be beyond absurdity, he realised. Yet it was there – in his heart; in his mind.

— How is my brave boy today? Bright-eyed and bushy-tailed, I hope, my love.

— Oh yes, Jeanette, I'm on top of the jolly old world, as you can see with those bifocals of yours.

He was anxious to hear what Johnny was saying to Eunice, but the nurse's twitterings would not grant him that favour.

— Mr Russell will be along very soon, my love. When he gives us the go-ahead, we'll take that nasty, nasty catheter away and pull some of those tubes out.

Forget the catheter, forget the tubes – they were secondary concerns to the man who was being denied the latest developments in the continuing tragedy of Johnny and Eunice.

The removal of Sunshine's catheter inspired Nurse Dunckley to new heights, or depths, of skittishness.

— Nothing much the matter with Harry's Mr Willy, is there? He'll be his usual self in a little while, my love.

You're a lucky Harry, you are. Only last week – or was it the week before? You lose all sense of time in here – only last week we had a nice young man in this very same bed who had to have a nasty, nasty catheter too, but in his case it was there for days on end. When we took it out, young Michael's Mr Willy had swelled up to the size of a vegetable marrow. The poor lad didn't know where to look, I swear, my love. Oh, it was that bloated. But your Mr Willy's the same chap he was on Thursday, I'm happy to report. He'll be a bit leaky for a while, but nothing to worry you unduly.

— How is Johnny? he asked when the gift of speech was restored to him.

— He's not one of my patients, Sunshine. But he's as well as can be expected.

'As well as can be expected' wasn't well enough, Harry Chapman learned from an overheard conversation between another doctor and another nurse in what he supposed was the late evening. A sudden, swift, wholly unexpected heart attack had dispatched the angry man whose leg had been amputated. It was a terrible shame, given that the rest of his body, waist up, had been functioning normally.

The saddened Harry Chapman was diminished by loss again, as he had been on Tuesday – was it Tuesday? – with the news that Iris Gibson, his sensible, cheerful comforter, had not survived the night. Iris had spoken to him, sensibly, from across the ward, but Jonathan Cooper had been out of his line of vision, as had the suffering Eunice, who was unable to give her husband or lover the immediate solace he craved. He wanted, now, to mourn them – the woman so determined to persuade the anonymous patient opposite her that she was only moderately unwell; the man grimly fantasising about his future as an entertainer at children's parties, impersonating Long John Silver with the parrot he'd trained to squawk 'Pieces of eight'. Harry Chapman could imagine the boys and girls, faces stained with chocolate, mouths bursting with cake and jelly, pretending to be terrified of the one-legged pirate with the talking bird on his shoulder. But their happy terror was not to be.

Harry Chapman hadn't heeded the ship-boy's warning on that October Saturday in 1982.

— Harry, I have fears for you.

The danger looming on his horizon was standing yards away, buying razor blades and shaving foam when Jack alerted him. Harry Chapman had recognised the heavily built man after only a moment's hesitation. He was in the presence of the middle-aged Ralph Edmunds, whom he had last confronted when the bully and the bullied were both sixteen. The gruff voice, deeper now, was almost the same as he remembered it, and the thick lips, and the ears that seemed to be pinned close to the head.

— Take care, Jack advised. — Take the greatest care.

Harry Chapman paid for the toothpaste and shampoo he had selected at an adjacent till. His eyes met those of the man he knew to be Ralph Edmunds.

— Do I know you? Do you know me?

— Yes. I was at school with you.

— You're Harry, aren't you?

— I am. And you're Ralph.

— That's me. Well, it's a small world.

— Yes, it is.

Jack, alert at his post, told Mister Harry to end the conversation and walk off, free, into the busy street.

— I saw your face in the paper once. I showed it to my mates at work and said you was in my class.

— Are you on your way somewhere, Ralph? Have you time for a drink?

— Always got time for a drink, Harry. If someone else's paying.

There was a pub nearby called the Tudor Rose. Its oak-beamed saloon bar reeked of stale beer and cigarettes and a lethal disinfectant, recently sprayed. The men's lavatory had been renamed Ye Knightes, the women's Ye Damsels, in the interests of historical authenticity.

— What will you have?

— Seeing as how you're paying, I'll have a whisky.

— Large?

— Why not?

They seated themselves at a corner table and clinked glasses.

— Cheers, Ralph.

— Bottoms up, Harry.

Ralph smirked, and said:

— Talk about a small world. Who'd have thought I'd bump into you? You're not as skinny as you used to be. Good living, eh?

— Good enough.

— Still at the writing lark?

— Yes. I've been teaching, too. I'm not long back from America. I was in Minnesota for a couple of years. And you? What's your job?

— I'm a gas fitter. Dirty work sometimes.

When Ralph excused himself and disappeared behind the door marked Ye Knightes, Jack whispered to Harry:

— Go now. Go while the going is good.

— I'll be careful, Jack.

Then Ralph returned, and Harry invited him to tell his story. Was he married, for instance?

— Was. 'Was' being the word. I got shot of the bitch. Do you smoke, Harry?

— No.

— Mind if I do?

— Not at all.

— We had a little girl. She must be twenty now.

— You don't see her?

— Only if I go to Spain. That's where her mother took her when we split up. She's been taught to hate me. Her mother's seen to that.

— Have you found another woman?

— Not looking, Harry. If I need a fuck, I buy a tart. When I've got some spare dosh to blow.

Ralph winked at Harry, and remarked again what a small world it was.

— You're not a woman man yourself, Harry. Is that true?

— It is.

— I guessed as much at school. Do you have a regular mate?

Harry Chapman, startling himself with his honesty, replied that he lived with a man who was far gone in gin and only stayed with him out of pity. He took his pleasures, such as they were, whenever and wherever he could find them.

— Sounds as if we're both lonely. I mean, you write books and I'm a gas fitter, but when push comes to shove, we're lonely bastards, aren't we, Skinny Boy? Remember me calling you Skinny Boy?

— Yes, Ralph.

Harry paid for a second round of drinks, despite Jack's cautioning speech as he did so.

— Very civil of you, Harry. Very civil indeed.

— My pleasure.

They talked, then, of schooldays, of Harry's perform-
ances as Emma Woodhouse and King Henry, of teachers
and fellow pupils.

— Are you happy, Ralph?

— A bit.

It was decided – Harry Chapman recalled as he lay awake
in the middle of the night with only the machines of healing for company – that the writer should treat the gas fitter
to dinner. In the Italian restaurant, Harry persuaded Ralph
to share a bottle of Chianti Classico.

— Wine's a drink for ponces, Harry. But, as it's you, I'll
try a drop.

They consumed two bottles and had a grappa each at the
end of the meal.

It was almost midnight when they left. As they made
their unsteady way towards Marble Arch, Harry explained
that, drunk as they were, Christopher would be drunker.

— My last train's gone, Skinny Boy. A taxi from here
will cost the bloody earth.

What madness, what alcohol-induced madness, possessed
Harry Chapman next? Bully and Bullied had stopped
outside a drab hotel.

— Shall we try here? Harry Chapman heard himself ask
the swaying Ralph Edmunds.

This was one of those establishments where no questions
were asked and no means of identification demanded. Cash
was all that was necessary to procure a double room on the
third floor.

The yawning receptionist handed him the key and said
that a Continental breakfast would be available between the
hours of seven and nine thirty. He recited this information
as if by rote, and then increased the volume on his transis-
tor. It was tuned to a foreign station: Harry heard, through

static, the sounds of a language – Slavic, perhaps – that he didn't recognise.

The room was as inviting as a coffin. Harry Chapman could not help but think of the lost souls who had taken refuge in its dinginess. Why was he here? Why was he here with his tormentor of decades past? Was he out of his mind?

— Christ, I'm pissed.

— So am I, Ralph.

He went into the bathroom. The bath was stained yellow and the porcelain chipped in places. There was a rusty shower connection and a plastic curtain.

He washed his face in cold water and dried himself with a rough towel.

His bully of yesteryear was undressing by the faint light of a bedside lamp with a pink shade. The body, Harry saw, was bulkier now, and the stomach had run to fat. Ralph was no classically perfect Adonis. His figure was less than Greek, was virtually misshapen, might even become gross with time.

What a small world it was and no mistake, what with him and clever Harry Chapman bumping into each other out of the blue and getting into the same bed together because they'd had a skinful, the pair of them, and what with their being the worse for wear and that was the truth of it in a nutshell . . .

Harry Chapman, naked, pulled back the bedspread and got between the sheets, which he doubted were totally clean. Soon Ralph Edmunds was lying alongside him in the darkness.

I am Ishmael, and he is Queequeg, the harpooneer, thought Harry Chapman, never at a loss for a connection between literature and life. Ralph doesn't carry a tomahawk and there's no trace of a scalp and he isn't adorned with decorative tattoos, but he is primitive in his way. So primitive, in fact, that the once-taunted Skinny Boy, with the fake Jewish cock, felt afraid and apprehensive. He realised he was too frightened to give his fear expression.

Then he heard Ralph snoring and reasoned that he was safe. Even so, he heard Jack beg him to make a speedy escape. But it was too late. Ralph was bound to wake up and ask what he was doing.

He dozed off, and what caused him to regain consciousness was the agonising pain he was enduring. Ralph was taking him with a fierce determination.

— This is what you want, you clever queer.

The clever, queer Harry Chapman wanted to scream, but stayed silent and immobile.

— You're a freak, Skinny Boy.

Ralph Edmunds let out what sounded like a cry of pleasure and bit his victim's ear. This, thought the captive beneath, is a sign of affection, or the nearest thing to it.

He remained still as death while Ralph washed himself in the bathroom.

Two or so hours later, he neither struggled nor protested when Ralph silently insisted on a repeat performance. His attacker was less ferocious and more relaxed and Harry Chapman sensed that he and the feared Ralph were experiencing mutual enjoyment.

— That's good, Harry whispered.

Towards morning, in the half-light, in the room with its patchy carpet and peeling flock wallpaper, Ralph set about his appointed task again when his unfondled, unkissed plaything returned to the bed after taking a lukewarm shower.

— God, was I drunk last night, said Ralph as he started to dress.

— Me too.

— There's a first time for everything, they say.

— Yes.

They left the hotel separately, Ralph having made his good-byes with another reference to the smallness of the world.

— Fancy me meeting clever old Skinny Boy of all people.

Harry saw that the sheets contained evidence of their sexual activity. The spilt semen had hardened and formed itself into what chambermaids call 'little maps of Ireland'. He counted three of them, and noted that there were traces of blood and shit as well.

As he journeyed homewards that Sunday morning, he remembered he had given Ralph his phone number in the restaurant.

— Good evening, Harry, my love.

(Somehow, at some hour of the previous day unknown to him, Harry Chapman had regained the blessed ability to speak.)

— Your love? I am not your love. Stop being silly.

— Temper, temper. Who's a grumpy Harry tonight? Your friend Jeanette is not going to take offence. She knows better than to do that.

— Does she really?

— She does, my love.

Why was this woman's vapid banter, with its ludicrous claims to a joint affection, objectionable to him in a way that Nancy Driver's trivial chit-chat wasn't? It was a question of character, he supposed. Nancy struck him as genuinely, inherently good, while Nurse Dunckley was a pretend-saint in starched uniform, a beacon of kindness dependent upon a supply of rechargeable batteries. Oh, these suppositions from the sickbed were probably facile, but they seemed accurate to him, for the moment.

— I'm sorry if I sounded curt, Nurse.

— Of course you are, my love.

The funeral of Harry Chapman was being held, surprisingly, in a church. It wasn't a Low Church either, but one
that was undeniably, even ostentatiously, High. Was his
send-off taking place, the dead man wondered, in a cathedral? And if so, which? A sudden glimpse of burnished gold
prompted him to think it was St Mark's in Venice.

Most of the mourners were already seated. Alice Chapman
stood out from the others because she was dressed in red, a
colour she never favoured for a host of reasons, chief of which
was exemplified in the two words 'scarlet woman'. Rose,
weeping softly in the row behind her sister, had donned
black for the occasion, in common with everyone else.
The Duchess of Bombay had smartened herself up in his
honour, which touched her deceased acquaintance. Prince
Myshkin, in the thick, hooded traveller's cloak he always
wore in northern Italy, was at her side. They were talking
earnestly, the Prince often nodding assent at her observations, and Harry strained to catch what they were saying.
The Duchess's witticisms, which seemed to be delighting
the unhappy Prince, were lost on Harry Chapman, whose
attention was now diverted by the arrival of Pamela, in a
hat D'Artagnan and his faithful musketeers might have
favoured, along with three friends he'd made when he was
an actor, each kitted out as characters from the *commedia
dell'arte*: Roberta, the comeliest Columbine ever; Gordon,
the zaniest Punchinello imaginable; and Ian, a brooding,
moody and menacing Harlequin.

Leo, looking plumply healthy, joined the throng, hand
in hand with Eleanor, his proud and loyal wife of four
decades and more. Philip Pirrip had journeyed from

Calcutta for this sad gathering, and so from the wilds of
Africa had King Babar and the veiled Queen Céleste, who
placed themselves discreetly in a pew that also contained
Jeoffrey, the immortal cat, who had licked his fur with
such dedication to feline duty that it glowed like jet or
some brilliant black diamond.

— I would prefer not to be present.

Harry Chapman, hearing the sepulchral voice, looked
about him for its owner. Bartleby was nowhere to be seen.

— Where are you, Bartleby?

— I would prefer to be absent from these proceedings.

— So should I, my lonely friend. So should I.

Suddenly, wonderfully, there was music. An unseen
orchestra was playing — in St Mark's? for Harry Chapman's
funeral? — Webern's orchestration of the fugue (*ricercata*)
from Bach's *The Musical Offering*.

— I chose this, the Duchess of Bombay confided in Prince
Myshkin. — This was my choice. Listen, listen. Every note
is like a jewel.

But Alice Chapman was of a different opinion, as she
soon made stridently clear to the man next to her.

— What a bloody racket.

Oscar Wilde, whose tainted name she had invoked
so many times in her son's childhood and youth, did not
respond. He inclined his head to sniff the green carnation
in his lapel and smiled to himself.

— You need to visit a barber.

The advice was unheeded and Alice Chapman muttered:

— I told Harry Chapman he would be late for his own
funeral one day, and here we are, sure enough, waiting
and waiting. He's making fun of us from beyond the
grave, if that's where he is, though I have to say I have
my doubts.

The glorious fugue stopped as suddenly as it had begun, and an eerie silence descended on the congregation as they faded from Harry Chapman's view.

He was convinced that Ralph would never contact him again. The scrap of paper on which he had written his phone number had been thrown out with the rubbish or screwed up into a ball and dropped into the gutter.

— There's someone calling you, Christopher shouted up the stairs. — Pick up the extension. He sounds like a moron.

Harry Chapman waited for the click that came when Christopher replaced the receiver before saying:

— Hello.

— Is that you, Harry?

— Yes.

— It's Ralph.

— You've taken a long time to call me. It must be over a year since we met by accident that afternoon.

— Do you want to see me again?

Jack, high up in the crow's nest, was silent.

— Yes.

— Same place? Saturday?

— Saturday's fine. Six o'clock at Green Park station. Is that convenient?

— Yes, Skinny Boy. That suits me.

They met. They went to a pub where the lavatories were designated Gentlemen and Ladies and talked inconsequentially. Ralph was still working as a gas fitter and Harry was still writing the same book he had been slaving over a year ago.

— I can miss my last train home if you want.

— Yes, I do.

— Let me remind you I'm a man, Harry, and don't you ever forget it.

— As if I would.

— Just in case you've got other ideas.

— Not at all.

— That's sorted then.

They ate and drank in a Lebanese restaurant, where Ralph was slightly disconcerted by the hot and cold *meze* Harry ordered. The food, he pronounced, was 'fiddly'. After the meal, they checked into another one-night cheap hotel. This establishment had pretensions to grandeur. It was cleaner than its grubby predecessor. The soap in the bathroom was scented with lavender, the favoured smell of his beloved Aunt Rose.

Ralph did not feign sleep and there was no declaration of drunkenness to excuse and account for his unnatural behaviour.

He surprised Harry in the shower, clutching Skinny Boy close to him and squeezing the breath out of his once-puny body. Ralph was asserting his brutish authority, but without his long-gone cronies to impress. The two of them were as they were on the day of the race in March 1950, but the game didn't end with Harry's being cast roughly aside. No, it had to continue now, take its logical course, as Harry had wanted it to and – Harry was quick to realise – as Ralph had hoped it would as well. The taunting of Leo Duggan, the jokes about circumcised cocks, the whooping and cheering of Ralph's followers, were camouflage for Ralph's real purpose – to dominate the school swot in the only way he knew and relished.

The game, the ritual, was to be replayed a dozen or more times during the next few years. Some of the one-night cheap hotels were cheaper than others, though none of them was as suicide-inducing as the very first setting for their late-flowering rapture. If Ralph was ever tempted to kiss his plaything, he kept the temptation in check, but fondling became acceptable to the man whose essential manhood Harry was forbidden to forget.

Harry Chapman looked forward to their liaisons, packing a small suitcase in advance with a change of socks and underwear, a fresh shirt perhaps, and his washbag, in case he felt like shaving in the morning. Ralph did the same. Their luggage was evidence of the overpowering passion they shared and gratified in anonymous rooms and suites on stolen Saturday nights.

One element, and one alone, was missing from these entanglements, Harry Chapman was shocked to acknowledge. The fear that had possessed him and, to be truthful, excited him when Queequeg had switched off the pink light and the tremulous Ishmael had lain expectantly beside him in the darkness was never to be replicated. Jack's warning whispers had been silenced. The anticipation of immediate pleasure was undiminished, but the terror – yes, he had felt terror in that seedy, flock-wallpapered room on the third floor – belonged now and for ever to the past.

— Good morning, Sunshine.
— Good morning to you, Doctor.
— Have you had a comfortable night?
— As far as I know, which isn't very much.
— You're on the mend, I'm happy to tell you.

Mr Russell and his team walked on, and Harry Chapman dreaded the imminent appearance of the ghoulish Nurse Dunckley. To his surprised relief, it was Nancy Driver who came to comfort him.

— Hello, Harry.

— Oh, Nancy, am I glad to see you.

— The feeling's mutual.

— What are you doing in here?

— You and your questions. I'm here, Mr Chapman, to give you the good news – good for us, that is – that you will be returning to the Zoffany Ward later today.

— Thank God.

— We'll expect a poem or two in exchange for our services.

— I'll try my best.

— That's our Harry. I'll leave you in peace now. Goodbye for the present.

He had survived for a whole week – was it, in fact, as long as that? – without a book or books. All he had read was the newspaper Pamela had given him, with the obituary of Leo, the kindest and most cultivated of his friends. Nothing else. He must be getting well again for what he craved now was the printed word.

It was the same craving he'd had in childhood. During his long silent convalescence, the nurses had brought him comics to look at.

One of them – her name was lost to memory, but her face would reassemble itself whenever he willed it – pointed at, and spoke, the funny words in the bubbles coming out of the mouths of Desperate Dan or Dennis the Menace. Back in the house near the gasworks and the candle factory, he gabbled their exclamations in his childish treble on the precious afternoons when his sister Jessie, returning from school, handed him the garishly coloured copies of the *Dandy* and the *Beano*, his first means of escape into the imagination.

— Take your head out of that rubbish. Your dinner's on the table.

— Just a minute, Mum.

— Enough of your minutes. That's how days and months and years go by with nothing done. Minutes add up, Harry Chapman.

Oh, the blessed days, months and years when Harry Chapman did nothing more adventurous than reading and wondering, the two in harmony with the old enemy Time out of sight and of no immediate concern to his giddily occupied mind.

The last hotel in which Ralph and Harry passed a night together was neither cheap nor dismal.

— You gone mad, Harry? This place is the lap of bloody luxury.

— Are you complaining?

— Can't say I am.

They breakfasted on scrambled eggs, toast, coffee, orange juice and champagne, brought to them in room 535 by a knowing Filipino, who winked at Harry when he signed the bill.

Ralph had never mentioned that he had a sister called Beryl. Harry Chapman heard of her existence when she phoned him some weeks after the assignation in luxurious surroundings. She had news for him, she announced ominously. He invited her to his home that evening.

— What a beautiful house you have, Mr Chapman.

— Thank you.

He led her into his study and brought her the glass of sherry she asked for. It was her one and only tipple, she confessed.

— What is your news, Beryl?

— I had to tell you face to face.

He waited.

— We're face to face.

— Ralph's dead. He did himself in. He did away with himself.

He wanted to know how and why, but was restrained from questioning her by embarrassment or tact – he couldn't decide which.

— He was very cut up, Beryl continued. — He found out his daughter Christine – she was the world to him – was in London, but she didn't wish to see him. That was the final straw, Mr Chapman –

— Harry, please –

— As I say, the final straw. The little cow, if you'll pardon my French, told him she hated his guts. I blame that cast-iron bitch of a wife of his. Mum and me warned Ralph that he was heading for trouble in spades if he went to the altar with Denise, but he wouldn't listen to us. 'Denise is the bee's knees,' he liked to joke. I haven't told her and Christine that he's gone. Let them find out for themselves if they're interested, which I bet they're not.

— Have you had the funeral?

— Yes, we have. Very quiet. Very private.

— I am so sorry, Beryl. I am so very sorry. What I don't understand is what you're doing here, why you've come to see me –

— It was his wish, Harry. It was in the note he left. He had a high regard for you. He said he was over the moon when he met you again after thirty years and what a small world it was that you were both in the same chemist's at the same time.

— You are kind, Beryl. I am touched by your kindness.

Beryl produced a sealed envelope from her handbag.

— This is for you, Harry, from Ralph. You open it when I leave. Ralph told me and Mum that you had more brains than were good for you when you were schoolboys.

— Did he, really?

— He really did.

Then Beryl said that Norman, her husband, would be in a tizzy because his supper wasn't on the table, and Terry, their bone-idle son, would be staring at the oven as if it was a spaceship from Mars. Typical men.

Harry Chapman kissed Beryl on both cheeks and she responded in kind.

— I'm afraid he hanged himself, Harry. In the stairwell of those awful bloody lodgings he ended up in. My lovely Ralph.

It was late in the evening when he opened the envelope. On a scrap of lined paper, Ralph had written:

Dear Harry

Words and myself dont get along but here goes. We got along fine we did with me doing something that took yours truly by surprise. I thank God it is a small world we live in. Here is a token of my esteem for you Harry and wear it to remember me. Your gas fitter mate and chum is getting out of it all.

Ralph

Underneath his signature, Ralph had added a solitary 'x'. An afterthought, perhaps? No, it was an expression of genuine affection.

Ralph's 'x', set down *in extremis*, denoted the kiss he had never conferred upon Harry; the kiss the clandestine lovers had been too wary or too frightened to share.

The token of Ralph's esteem was a ring that was too large for even the thickest of Harry's fingers.

Sunday

— WELL, YOU'RE A survivor, Harry Chapman. I'll say that much for you. Not like your father, who gave up the ghost between two blinks of an eye.

— That's a monstrous thing to say. Dad was worn out, and with good reason. He fought in the Flanders trenches, Mother, in case you've forgotten. Private 36319. I'm still here thanks to the advances in medicine that have been made in the sixty years since his death.

— I didn't ask for a lecture.

— You're getting one just the same. If Dad were alive now, and ill, and in this hospital, the chances are that he would be lying where I am, listening to you telling him that he's a survivor –

He opened his eyes and within minutes was aware that he had been transported – somehow, at some time unknown to him – back to the Zoffany Ward. It was almost like being home.

— I'm the welcoming committee, Harry, said Marybeth Myslawchuk. — Your other friends have the day off.

— Which day is it?

— Sunday. And a pretty wet and chilly one at that.

— I think I need something to read.

— I can get you a paper.

— I'd prefer a book.

— I'll see what I can find.

The beds on either side of him were unoccupied. He felt strangely sad not to have the company of the infirm at close hand.

— You could always picture me, spewing up blood.

— No, Christopher. Please rest in peace.

— Not while you're alive I won't. I'm here to gnaw at your guilty conscience.

— My guilty conscience? You were hell-bent on self-destruction.

— And you were the ideal accomplice. You more than aided me in my mission to wipe Christopher Riley off the face of the earth.

This was a patent untruth, since it was the pitying Harry Chapman who had nursed the ungrateful Christopher during his final, gin-free illness. He had wanted the man who had declared and delivered his obsessive love for him twenty-two years earlier to go on living, and to be well enough, what's more, to go on living alone, with his victim Harry safely stowed elsewhere.

— You left it too late to show you cared a fig for me.

Christopher had died in the spring of 1986. His face, in death, was as serene as any saint's. A stranger, looking down at him, would have marvelled at his composure, for there was no indication that this was a man who had been consumed with loathing for most of the people he'd encountered in his forty-eight years. There was no hint, either, of the self-hatred that had borne him, inexorably, to the morgue.

Harry Chapman gave his becalmed tormentor a last kiss on the forehead and, days later, organised a grand secular funeral for him. The crematorium chapel was crowded with those of his friends and acquaintances who had endured and survived his displeasure. They recalled his wit, his early promise of success as a theatrical designer, as they listened to the snatches of Mozart that replaced the expected hymns and lessons. Harry read from Jane Austen – Mr Collins informing Elizabeth Bennet that he would honour her with his hand in marriage, and Captain Wentworth writing a hasty, desperate letter to Anne Elliot, the woman he had loved and lost, and was to love again, for ever more: 'I must speak to you by such means as are within my reach. You pierce my soul. I am half agony, half hope. Tell me not that I am too late, that such precious feelings are gone for ever. I offer myself to you again with a heart even more your own than when you broke it, eight and a half years ago . . .'

The following week Harry Chapman handed over the casket containing the ashes of the man who had loved him with an unbearable intensity to Christopher's brother Martin, who was happily married and the father of three well-adjusted children.

— I'll have our mother's grave opened and Chris and she can be reunited. He was the apple of her eye, not me.

Martin spoke without bitterness. Susan Riley's devotion to her firstborn was a fact, and as such had to be acknowledged.

— I called him The Fuse when we were kids. He was always blowing up and going into a long silent sulk if you didn't respond. I have to confess to you, Harry, that seeing him twice a year was once too often for me. Perhaps Mum was right to be so attentive to him. I honestly believe that he came into the world unhappy and couldn't wait to get out of it. What amazes me is that he managed to take so long to achieve his ambition.

Harry Chapman thought, but didn't say, that Christopher gave those closest to him the gift of his misery. He had been a recipient, as were those whom Christopher had chosen before him — the very same escapees who turned up at Mortlake to lament his passing.

— Be completely free now, Harry. Come and see us soon.

— I will, Martin.

Twenty and more years afterwards, Harry Chapman would like to boast that he was completely free of the late Christopher Riley. But of course he wasn't, and could never be. In that first decade of his freedom, he would often wake in the night with the sound of Christopher's taunts and recriminations echoing in his brain. He was usually abject as a consequence, pleading with his bloated accuser to be really and truly dead.

— Die, die, die, he'd moan, hearing the anguish in his heart and mind.

There were no relics of Christopher in the house — his clothes had been deposited with a Third World charity; each and every photograph of him had been cut into tiny shreds; his designs had gone to a museum where they were seldom put on display. All physical reminders of his malign presence were scattered elsewhere. Yet something of him — his spirit, was it? — remained.

— You tried to eliminate me, you piece of shit, but you didn't succeed.

— I'm afraid I didn't.

— May you rot in hell.

— Is that your home these days?

— I'm not telling you. That's my secret. You'll be able to answer the question yourself very soon now.

Oh God, if You exist, spare me Christopher Riley's company in heaven or hell or purgatory, Harry Chapman, who was unaccustomed to praying, prayed. He repeated the prayer, silently as before, in his desperation.

— There was the Brahms afternoon, Pamela reminded him. — I was with you, Harry. We had the merriest lunch, my dear. And then we went shopping. And you suddenly said you were in the mood for Brahms, Brahms and more Brahms. So we went to one of the big record stores and you bought –

— I bought the four symphonies, the two piano concertos, the violin concerto, the double concerto, the clarinet quintet, the *German Requiem*, the string sextets, the Intermezzi Opus 117, violin sonatas and lieder galore. I took them home and feasted on them for weeks on end. Christopher had hated Brahms's music for a reason or reasons he disdained to vouchsafe. It was enough that he hated it. Brahms was 'heavy'; close of argument.

In April 1986, the ban on Brahms was lifted and the house in Hammersmith resonated with the sounds Harry Chapman had only been able to enjoy in concert halls or in his apartment in Sorg, Minnesota. While Christopher lived, Mozart prevailed, though Harry was permitted to listen to his beloved Schubert if Christopher was in a lenient or forgiving mood.

— You're welcome here, Johannes.

— Who's that, Harry?

— I was meandering, Marybeth.

— I've brought you a well-thumbed paperback. It won't be up to your exalted standards, I fear.

— Don't worry. Any trash will do.

But any trash wouldn't do, as he discovered after reading thirty pages of *Operation Midas*, a crime novel by someone called Rick Jewell. Its principal character, an international fraudster working under the archly comic sobriquet

Cambio Wechsel, is scheming and dealing in Milan, Las Palmas, Geneva and the City of London within the course of a single paragraph. Cambio is a Robin Hood for our time, it is implied, robbing and even killing the rich to aid the poor. He has an assistant, the nubile Melissa, who tempts corrupt and priapic financiers into her bed, and then . . . and then . . .

— Would you care for a bite to eat?

— Yes, I think I would, he replied to the stranger with a trolley.

— Fried plaice or chicken curry?

— I'll try the plaice.

— It's as good as anything we have.

There was apple crumble and ice cream to follow, and coffee or tea.

— I like my tea very weak. Is that possible?

— I'd say not.

— Coffee, then.

He ate the fish and peas and dessert and drank the tasteless coffee. He lay back in the bed and cursed Rick Jewell and everyone who wrote badly for enormous gain and wished – how he wished – that Graham was by his side.

— Tell me about my grandfather, Dad.

— I wish I could, son. I was barely four when he died. All I remember of him is that he stammered. Or is it stuttered? He called me F-F-F-F-Frank whenever he spoke to me. He was known as Stammering or Stuttering Sammy. He was a carpenter by trade.

— Hello, H-H-H-H-Harry.

— Hello, Grandad.

— N-N-N-Nice to m-m-m-meet you at l-l-last.

Harry Chapman, opening his eyes, looked for the long-dead stammerer and saw Nancy Driver beaming at him.

— Marybeth tells me you've been reading.

— Reading? No, I was looking at words. For an entire, wasted hour.

— Such ingratitude, joked Marybeth, who made a request for a Shakespeare sonnet to charm her ears before she went off duty, if that wasn't too tall an order.

— Give me a moment or two. Let me set my tired old brain in motion. Do you have a favourite?

Marybeth answered that it was so far back in time that she'd studied the glorious Bard, as her teachers in Winnipeg nicknamed him, that she couldn't rightly remember ever having a favourite. She was happy for the amazing Harry Chapman to decide.

Why – he asked himself once he was in full flow – had he chosen this particular one of the one hundred and fifty-four sonnets he had committed to memory in his late youth and early manhood? Had he come at last to the belief that the earth is sinful? Was his own body, harbouring his own poor soul, nothing more than a fading mansion fit only for worms to inherit? Yet he could say 'Within be fed, without be rich no more' with a conviction that was lacking in the man of twenty.

— *And death once dead, there's no more dying then.*

— If that came true, we'd all be out of a job, Nancy Driver observed with a wry smile. — We'd have to find something else to occupy our time, wouldn't we, Marybeth?

— I don't think we have the looks or the figures to make the transition from on-call girls to call girls, do you?

Maciek Nazwisko interrupted them to say that one of the two vacant beds would soon be occupied by an elderly gentleman called Mr Breeze.

— He'll be company for you, Harry. Or shall we hide you behind the curtain?

— I'll tell you later, Nancy.

Perhaps Mr Breeze had been released, or perhaps he had died somewhere downstairs, for there was no sign of the elderly gentleman when Harry Chapman awoke from an undisturbed sleep.

— You seem flustered.

— I was expecting to see someone in the next bed.

— You'll have to wait. There's been a delay. He has to take another test.

It was only after she had left that he realised he'd been talking to Veronica. He had momentarily forgotten her name.

— Veronica, Veronica, he whispered to himself.

This sudden, brief lapse of memory reminded him of the last time he saw Aunt Rose alive. She was as happy as she'd ever been, but now her glowing optimism was set on a future that had been the past for nearly a century. She burbled to him about the other naughty girls in the village-school playground and the only name he recognised was that of his mother, Alice. Of Gertie, who was especially mischievous, he knew nothing, and Eliza, Martha and Rhoda were merely shadows. She spoke of, and to, her vanished Bartrip relations, most of whom had shuffled off their mortal coils long before Harry Chapman had become entrapped in his. She smiled at a point beyond her nephew as they sat on the little terrace outside her room in the Eventide Home. He might have been, and indeed was, anyone but the Harry she had loved and encouraged. They drank tea and nibbled on ginger biscuits, and he commanded himself not to weep as she went on smiling at something or someone it was impossible for him to see.

— Gertie, Gertie, Mrs Clarke is going to smack you for getting your hands and face so grubby.

He found himself unable to respond. Should he try to communicate with the invisible Gertie? The question was answered as he was forming it. He stayed silent.

The 'stranger to moodiness', as her brother-in-law had deemed her, continued to smile and nod. She hummed a snatch of a song once, which vaguely resembled 'Alexander's Ragtime Band'. She let out a fusillade of farts, and neither acknowledged nor apologised for the noise and the rancid odour.

He rose slowly from the wicker chair.

— Auntie, I must catch my train back to London.

— And now it's Eliza, would you believe, who's making mischief.

He waited to learn the precise nature of Eliza's mischievousness, but Aunt Rose was not ready to divulge it.

He took her hands and kissed them. He said goodbye. He tried to stare into her eyes. Whatever they were seeing did not include him.

He left her with Gertie, Eliza, Martha, Rhoda and the child Alice; with the Bartrips of long ago; with the staff of the Eventide Home, who brought her food and drink and helped to wash and dress her.

He left her without her nephew Harry Chapman and, it occurred to him, her niece Jessie. He walked towards the small country station in a haze of tears.

The bed on his right-hand side was occupied by a snoring man who was bald except for a single tuft of reddish hair that stood up from his scalp like a question mark. He

assumed him to be the Mr Breeze Maciek had mentioned
earlier.

— Is that Mr Breeze? he asked Veronica, who was tending to the new patient.

— It is indeed.

— I think I've seen him somewhere before.

— In a pub, more than likely. I'm sorry, Harry, I didn't
say that. I was speaking out of turn.

— I didn't hear you.

Mr Breeze's snores came to an abrupt close. He seemed to
have the gift of being able to open one eye at a time. It was
a solitary eye that stared at Harry Chapman.

— Who? Where?

— Mr Breeze?

— Who wants to know? Are you a tax collector? My
landlord? A detective?

— No. My name's Harry Chapman. I write books.

— Have I heard of you?

— Perhaps. Or perhaps not.

— I gave up on reading when I reached fifty, didn't I?
Mr Breeze's other eye leapt open as he spoke.

— Did you?

— I did. That's when I opted for the Book of Life instead,
wasn't it?

— Was it?

— It was. What's your name again?

— Harry Chapman.

— Harry Chapman, eh? Harry Chapman? Did you write
a novel about old age when you were very young?

— Yes.

— I was on the literary scene myself, economically
speaking you might say, some while back, in the whirling
mists of time.

— Tell me more, Mr Breeze.

— Randolph Breeze is my name, isn't it? I'm 'Breezy' for short, but 'Randy' I simply will not countenance, under any circumstances. Is that understood? I've been known to one and all as 'Breezy' since I was a boy, haven't I?

— You said you were on the literary scene.

— I was, indeed. I trained as an accountant, like my father before me, and his before him. I worked in the accounts department of a famous publishing house. If I say, as I shall, that the great poet Thomas Stearns, alias T. S., Eliot was on the board of directors, you will guess which house I mean. Yes?

— Yes.

— I stayed in that job for five years or more. Happy at my post, wasn't I?

— Were you?

— I was. But then, disaster struck.

The man who liked to be known as Breezy paused for dramatic effect. Harry Chapman was delighted to feed him his cue:

— Disaster?

— Too strong a word, you would be right in thinking. It wasn't an earthquake, a flood or any other accident of God. No, I was fired, Mr Chapman. Sacked. On the spot. Told to pick up my things and go.

— For what reason?

— Insobriety. I was prone to partake of what are known in the trade as 'liquid lunches'. On the disastrous afternoon in question, I returned to the office several half-seas over. I was monumentally arseholed. Could I defend my behaviour? No, I couldn't. But Dame Fortune was on my side, as she has been so often in the past. She led me to the men's washroom.

— Did she?

— She certainly did. I was ridding myself of some of the vast quantity of stout and whisky chasers I'd imbibed, when who should come through the door but T. S. Eliot himself. He wished me good day and disappeared into a cubicle. But not before depositing his teeth in a mug by the washbasin. You can imagine, can't you, how my heart leapt at the sight of the genius's dentures? I hadn't a moment to lose. I removed those pearly white beauties from the mug, wrapped them in my none-too-clean handkerchief and fled 24 Russell Square as fast as my shaky pins could carry me.

— Are you saying, Mr Breeze, that you stole T. S. Eliot's teeth?

— I am saying precisely that. You see that small case, that valise, poking out from my locker? They're inside. I keep them in tip-top condition by polishing them with a couple of squirts of bleach once a week.

— You never thought of returning them to him?

— The idea crossed my mind and went on walking. A man who has been awarded the Nobel Prize in Literature could surely afford a second, or third, pair of gnashers. Would you like to buy them off me? I've no one to leave them to.

— I don't think I have need of them, thank you very much, Mr Breeze.

— I'm offering them to you at a knock-down price. Five hundred?

— No, no.

— I can accept four, maybe? At a pinch?

— Not from Harry Chapman, I'm afraid.

— I could have sold them a thousand times, but I didn't, did I?

— That was very noble of you.

When Veronica next appeared, Harry asked her for protection. He needed the curtain between himself and the loquacious Mr Breeze.

— I understand. I understand very well.

Harry Chapman arrived at the party breathless. He had climbed an interminable marble staircase in order to reach the festivities, which were now in full sway. This last was the appropriate word, since most of those who had been invited were swaying. A white-jacketed waiter, who looked not unlike Dr Pereira, handed him a glass of flat champagne with the words:

— The bubbles made their excuses and left.

He decided to mingle with the crowd. Everyone present had a sizeable name tag fixed to their lapels, so it was easy to identify the various guests. A weasel-faced man with a lock of black hair stuck to his forehead and watery dark eyes was Herr Joseph Roth, who described himself as a depressed wandering Jew who had a mad wife somewhere, wrote books for a pittance and died of liver failure. Beside him was the bespectacled, mustachioed Senhor Fernando Pessoa, who also cared to be known as Alvaro de Campos, a naval engineer educated in Glasgow, Ricardo Reis, a classical pagan, and the rustic intellectual Alberto Caeiro. 'I have never loved anyone, not even my three other selves' his card proclaimed. He, too, had a liver that failed him.

He noticed, in passing, a stocky middle-aged man by the name of Mr Malcolm Lowry. 'I killed myself when I was forty-eight, but my body had already died on me' was the message he conveyed to the other partygoers, such as James Joyce and a shyly smiling man in a dinner suit who said that he had posed as a successful business entrepreneur who sold lavatory bowls and brewery equipment but his real work, the work that killed him, was writing. He was in this haunted ballroom for the same reason as Herr Roth, Senhor Pessoa, Messrs Lowry and Joyce – the drink, the demon drink.

— It's the Mexican day of the dead today, drawled Mr Lowry. — Strike up the band.

And a band struck up with an eerie funeral dance. A host of skeletal dancers came into view, led by Mr Randolph Breeze, who held T. S. Eliot's upper and lower dentures in his right hand, playing them as if they were half of a pair of castanets.

He saw that he was still curtained off. It was just as well, for it seemed that Mr Breeze had a visitor.

— You haven't come to nag me, have you, Blanche?

— No, Randolph, I haven't. I will say this, though. A man of your age and chronic state of health shouldn't be drinking himself into a stupor. Do you have any recollection of what you got up to last night?

The ever-curious Harry Chapman waited long minutes for Randolph's reply.

— Well, have you?

— I met you at seven, Blanche. Is that correct?

— It is. I gave you an envelope, if you recall.

— Yes, Blanche, I do.

— What did it contain?

— You know what. Money. A temporary loan. To tide me over, yes?

— To pay your overdue rent.

— That, too.

— Tell me what happened to you after I left.

— After you left?

— After I left.

— I stayed on for another drink, didn't I?

— And another, and another, I should imagine. You were found in the street with your face in the gutter.

— That can't be true. Was I?

— It is true and you were.

— I had my valise with me, didn't I?

— Yes, Randolph. It's safe and sound. I can see it from here.

— Face in the gutter, Blanche?

— Some decent soul, some Good Samaritan, called for an ambulance. That's why you're in hospital.

In the silence that followed this revelation, Harry Chapman hoped that Breezy and the unseen Blanche would entertain him further.

— Blanche, have you heard of Harry Chapman?

— The novelist? Yes, of course I have. I've read at least three of his books. Why do you ask?

— He's in the next bed. Asleep, I think. Imagine meeting him in a public ward.

— Have you talked to him?

— Oh, yes. We've more than talked. He's a soulmate, Blanche. He's made me an offer for my most treasured possession.

— Are you joking? The false teeth?

— He recognises them for what they are – a unique relic of literary history. He's prepared to pay me five hundred smackers.

— Then he's a bloody fool.

— It means I'll be able to pay back your loan.

Harry Chapman, enraptured by the conversation, added to the entertainment by moaning softly. The acting skills he'd acquired in his youth were reaping a peculiar benefit now.

— He's waking up, said Randolph. — We'd best be careful what we say.

— Why is that? Because you were lying? As usual.

The curtains were parted abruptly and a pink-faced, white-haired woman appeared at the foot of Harry Chapman's bed.

— Mr Chapman?

— Yes, he responded, weakly.

— Are you interested in buying T. S. Eliot's teeth from that old rascal Randolph Breeze?

Harry stared back at the woman.

— Leave him alone, Blanche, shouted Randolph. — Stop pestering him, can't you? Can't you see he's a very sick man?

— Is it true, Mr Chapman?

— What day is it, Nurse? I've lost all sense of time.

— I'm sorry, Mr Chapman. Go back to sleep. I enjoyed your novels.

She drew the curtain and he was cocooned again.

— May God forgive you, Blanche Westermere, for I never shall.

— God? What do you know of God? And as for God's forgiveness, I'll need it, Randolph Breeze, after all the years I've spent trying to rescue you from the bottomless bloody pit you keep digging for yourself.

— I didn't mean it, Blanche. It just came out. Please, Blanche.

But Blanche had stormed off, and Harry was pleased that the farce had come to such a satisfactory end.

'Some lose the day with longing for the night, and the night in waiting for the day': how Harry Chapman wished that he'd heeded Jeremy Taylor's wise observation more conscientiously, more often. He vowed to himself that if, and when, he was released from this timeless place, he would occupy each waking hour with fruitful activity. He had made this vow before and had failed to keep it. Those hours ahead of him were precious now because he could envisage an end to them.

Jack, the ship-boy, lithe and alert as ever, called down from the crow's nest:

— You have work to finish, Harry.

— I know I have.

— I will keep a close watch for you.

Harry Chapman — forcing his own skinny body out of King Henry's vast gold robe; pulling off Henry's Plantagenet wig; easing Henry's beard from his face; and stepping out of Henry's shoes after the final performance — saw the ageless Jack in his cotton clothes and knew he had a friend for all his life, however short, however long, it was to be.

— You are the first character I can remember inventing. You were Shakespeare's to begin with, but then I made you my own. I gave you flesh and blood.

— You did what, Harry Chapman? Who are you boasting to? If I recall aright, it was me who gave you flesh and blood and no one else.

— You're quite right, Mother. Thank you.

— Don't you forget.

The friendlier voice of Sister Nancy Driver asked him how he was feeling, as she felt his pulse and checked his blood pressure.

— The better for seeing you. A cliché, I know, but I mean it.

— Mr Breeze left while you were sleeping. I expect you're relieved, aren't you?

— I suppose I am.

— He was a bit tetchy. He wanted to say goodbye to you. He said he had some important business of a special nature to do with you.

Harry Chapman laughed.

— What's so funny?

— Mr Randolph Breeze – known to his friends as Breezy, but certainly not Randy – had plans to sell me T. S. Eliot's teeth.

— Your own teeth are perfectly good.

So Harry Chapman recounted to the slightly confused Nancy Driver the story of how Mr Breeze became the illegal owner of a major poet's dentures.

— He offered to sell them to me, but I refused politely.

— I'm afraid Mr Breeze is a typical example of the kind of patients we get in here at weekends. Let's hope his lady friend Blanche leads him away from the bottle for a while. What she sees in him is a mystery.

A mystery, Harry Chapman did not say, which he'd attempted to unravel throughout his writing life. The ludicrous Randolph and the hapless Blanche were a part of that unsolvable enigma.

He could hear two voices – one sharp and abrasive, the other refined to the point of haughtiness. Both speakers were women. They were somewhere in the ward. That much was clear to him.

— I have no time to waste on the tittle-tattle of servants.

— What's 'tittle-tattle' when it's at home? Struggling to keep body and soul together isn't tittle-tattle in my book.

— Which book is that, may one ask? Does it contain words, perchance?

— Perchance it does, perchance.

The caustic voice belonged to Alice Chapman, but who was the snooty, condescending woman who was reluctant to converse with her?

— Is there no escaping the mongrels in one's midst?

No, no, it couldn't be. It was Virginia Woolf who used the term 'mongrel' to describe working men and women. Other writers of her class and period referred to the 'lower orders' or 'hoi polloi', but 'mongrel' was, as far as he knew, her coinage.

— I've been called some names by the likes of the la-di-da but nobody's ever said I was a mongrel. A mongrel's a dog that's a bit of this and a bit of that, and I don't see how it applies to yours truly Alice Chapman, Bartrip that was.

— You are being excessively tiresome. I must insist that you return to your quarters, or wherever it is you belong.

— You can insist as much as you want, Mrs Woolf, but I'm staying exactly where I am. I'm not stirring from my Harry's side just to suit your convenience. The boy needs me.

— Oh, how you creatures breed, sighed the famous novelist. — Another ragamuffin to swell your already over-crowded ranks.

He could hear his mother seething before she responded:

— My friend Nellie Boxall warned me about you. She said you could be a high-and-mighty cow when you had the mood to be. Well, don't expect me to empty your chamber pot, milady. We creatures, as you call us, have our dignity and there are limits as to what you can tell us to do. You may think your shit's superior to ours, but it stinks just the same.

— The coarseness. The vulgarity.

'The humanity', Harry Chapman wanted to intervene, but kept his counsel. Was it possible that his mother had once worked in a menial capacity for Mr and Mrs Woolf? If so, she had never talked of the experience to her children Jessie and Harry. But here she was, standing up for the rights she didn't possess, arguing with the author who had bleached the English novel of all the vibrant colours her predecessors had imbued it with.

— Come on, Ma. Teach her a lesson.

— Speak when you're spoken to, Harry Chapman. I brought you up to have good manners. I won't have you disgracing me.

— I'm sorry I interrupted.

— You should be. Now, where was I? Ah yes, my duties. Washing, cleaning and cooking. Was there anything else Your Ladyship required?

— Yes, there is. I require you to be silent in your endeavours.

— In my what?

— Your tasks. The trivial chit-chat of underlings distracts me from my work.

— You're not much of a listener, are you? I mean to say, Charles Dickens never stopped listening.

This was a surprise to Harry Chapman – not just the accuracy of his mother's literary criticism, but the discovery that at some point in her life she had read one, at least, of the Inimitable's novels. It had been her custom in his youth to remark ad infinitum that reading books gave people the wrong sort of ideas and caused them to go blind in later life.

— We have haddock and sausage meat for dinner. Have them ready for the table at seven o'clock sharp, if you please.

— Haddock and sausage meat? You toffs have some funny tastes, I must say. Haddock and sausage meat – I never heard the like. What a combination.

— Your views on our culinary predilections are neither apposite nor welcome. To the kitchen with you, Chapman. Forthwith.

— Do I steam the haddock and fry the sausage meat, Mrs Hoity-Toity? Or do I shove the bleeders in a stewpot?

— You are worse than the Person from Porlock with your inane opinions and ridiculous questions.

To judge by the silence that followed, it would seem that the writer had had the last word. Having the last word was an art form that Alice Chapman had mastered after several decades of practice. It was unlike her to be cowed into abject submission.

— You'll be in for a fine surprise when you see what I've done with your haddock and sausage meat. The kitchen is out of bounds to you while Alice Chapman, Bartrip that was, is cooking in it. I'll do my work and you'll do yours and that's the last word on the subject.

His mother had triumphed, as he knew and hoped she would. She slammed the door shut in celebration. The slamming of doors was her other artistic feat. No one ever slammed a door with such deadly conviction.

Someone must have opened a window because a chill wind swept through the ward. Harry Chapman wrapped the blanket tight about him, but the cold persisted.

A woman was speaking in a quiet, grieving voice. A man, not far from her, was weeping inconsolably.

— We were reading the story of Lancelot and Guinevere together. So moved were we by their love – their forbidden love – that we found ourselves embracing each other and kissing. Love was commanding us to kiss, to enjoy ourselves. Oh, Harry, it was the happiest afternoon of my life and now I recall it in misery.

The man's cries of pain heightened in intensity.

Harry Chapman tried to console Francesca by saying that he already knew what happened later that radiant afternoon. The man who was sharing those ardent kisses with her was the handsome Paolo, the younger brother of her husband Gianciotto Malatesta. Francesca had a daughter and Paolo was the father of two boys, but now they were in the throes of a passion beyond language or sense. They were still in a state of timeless bliss when Gianciotto surprised them. Drawing his sword, he rushed to kill his brother, but Francesca intervened and was stabbed through the heart. She died as Gianciotto dispatched her lover in his fury.

— Love brought us to our death.

Was it Sister Nancy or Marybeth Myslawchuk who was ordering the unhappy Paolo to stop sobbing? There were very sick people here who were on the brink of dying and they needed rest and quiet at this crucial time in their lives. They had their sorrows, too.

In the middle of the night – for such he imagined it was – Harry Chapman lay awake and thought of the maverick American composer Charles Ives. He tried to picture him in his home in New England, seated at his piano one day in 1926. He had just completed a song called 'Sunrise', but that title was too hopeful, too optimistic, because Ives had just reached a conclusion that was bitter to him. He closed the lid of the piano in the knowledge that his gift was gone.

He left his music room and went downstairs to join his wife. (Was Harry Chapman right in thinking that her name was Harmony?) She asked him why he was crying, and when he had recovered sufficiently he told her the grim news.

He was fifty-two when he announced, correctly, that his ability to compose had vanished. He was to live another twenty-eight years – almost as long as the life of Schubert – with no new sounds in his head. He often marvelled that Beethoven, in his deafness, could do what he was unable to do, with wondrous results.

So Harry Chapman, the man of sometimes inspired suppositions, supposed.

Monday

HIS MORNING ABLUTIONS were done. Maciek Nazwisko had helped him to wash and shave and his visit to the lavatory had passed without problems. He had drunk a moderately weak cup of tea and eaten two slices of toast with strawberry jam. With Mr Randolph Breeze in mind, he had recited Eliot's 'Preludes' from memory to his usual group of poetry lovers. Dr Pereira had commented on Harry's improving health and said that he should be free to leave in a few days.

— Unless you have a setback, but at the moment that doesn't seem likely.

— You give me hope.

The doctor smiled his fruitseller's smile and went off to examine a newly arrived patient.

— Harry, you are a prize cunt. I thought we were friends.

— We are, Wilf.

— Then why, why did I have to hear from that old bitch Pamela Kenworth that you were in hospital? You could have let me know you were poorly.

— I didn't want any fuss. Take a seat. Thanks for coming.

— Christ, I hate these places. I've been inside too many of them. They all smell the same. It doesn't matter if it's an expensive clinic or a dump like this, there's always that peculiar stench. It hit me as soon I came in at the main entrance.

— I've been too preoccupied to notice any smells, Harry lied. — Given your horror of hospitals, it's truly noble of you to be sitting here with me.

— What with my prostate scare and my cataracts and my diabetes and my irregular heartbeat I think my horror, as you rightly call it, is justified.

— Absolutely. How are you feeling at the moment?

— The prostate hasn't been sorted yet, and as you can see, the cataracts have been removed, one after the other, and now my doctor has put me on four milligrams of rat poison a day to stop me having a stroke. Apart from that, I'm as well as can be expected.

— You look healthy.

— Appearances are deceptive, not to say misleading. If I appear healthy, Harry, it's only on the surface.

— I'm sorry to hear that.

— No sorrier than I am to have to tell you. The removal of the cataracts was a nightmare. The surgeon – if that's the proper word for the cack-handed so-and-so – pierced a vein on his first attempt, which meant that I couldn't see for blood. God, was I angry. I'd waited an eternity for the simple operation and now I had to go on waiting. I've been in the wars lately, Harry.

— It certainly sounds like it.

— To cap everything else, I now have three stents keeping my arteries open. Three, can you believe?

Harry Chapman listened enraptured to Wilfred Granger's soliloquy, which catalogued his every complaint. His eyes, his heart, his prostate were failing him, and his recently detected diabetes ensured that he was unable to drown his ever-present sorrows, as he was accustomed to, with a generous nightly intake of wine. His ingrowing toenail was given due attention, as was his inability to masturbate.

— Can that really be the time?

Wilfred Granger consulted his watch with feigned surprise.

— An hour passes so quickly in the company of an old friend. Harry, I must be making tracks. I have a lunch appointment on the other side of London and I'm already running late. Don't forget to phone me as soon as you're home again.

— I shan't forget. It was kind of you to come today.

— It's always a pleasure seeing you.

Harry Chapman had known Wilf since the 1960s, when he'd played Third Witch in the *enfant terrible*'s controversial production of *Macbeth*. 'There is no earthly reason why the Witches have to be women,' Wilf had announced at the first rehearsal. 'And what's more, I don't think they're Scottish either.' What were they then? Harry and his fellow crones wondered. 'Let's make them monks.' Monks? 'Franciscan monks. Very devout, and very close to nature.' The First Witch protested, 'But they are called witches, Wilf.' 'By the ungodly Macbeths,' Wilf riposted.

Wilf Granger's 'pioneering' interpretation was lauded by the same critics who praised Hal Musgrave's 'revolutionary' *Hamlet*, in which the gloomy Dane was portrayed as the crazed inheritor of congenital syphilis. Hal was Wilf's keenest rival for a decade – each outwitting the other in their novel 'exhumations' (Hal's word) of Shakespeare's tragedies. Hal's all-black *Othello*, with the Moor of Venice the solitary white presence on stage, was considered prophetic in 1969, and in a curious sense it was. The rivalry ended with Hal's accidental death later that year, overdosing on heroin.

Harry Chapman remembered, now, the joyous occasion when the First Witch or Monk asked the director why a devout Franciscan would shriek 'I come, Graymalkin!'

'Oh, Terence, you have such a restricted imagination. You say, not shriek, "Brother Graymalkin" or "Father Graymalkin" instead. And you, Andrew, will substitute "Brother Paddock calls". Is that clear?'

The Three Monks, stifling incipient hysteria, nodded.

Wilfred Granger was another survivor. He had outlived four – or was it five? – tempestuous marriages. He had been a Roman Catholic, to please (and guarantee sexual contact with) his first wife; a sabre-rattling atheist; an insufferably smug Buddhist; an all-things-to-all-men agnostic; and latterly, and gloriously, a hypochondriac with a pathological interest in his own decay. He had abandoned the theatre in his fifties, and assumed the role of guru to younger directors and actors who considered his very short book, *Merely Players*, a fount of theatrical wisdom. It had attracted thousands of international worshippers to come and sit at his expensively shod feet. His unwavering self-love was the abiding reason why Harry Chapman was fond of him, knowing as Harry did that it's the most inadequate love of all – Wilf's insatiable need for it could never be satiated, never gratified.

And, at seventy-six, he still wore his dusty grey hair tied in a ponytail.

— Oh, Jessie, you haven't had much of a life.

— Who says so, Harry?

They were standing on either side of Alice Chapman's coffin. The undertaker had only just closed the lid on her, with her children's permission.

— This isn't the time or the place to talk about me.

— I suppose not.

He broached the subject of Jessie's ill-fated existence some weeks later and was startled by her response.

— You have a nerve, Harry. I know you've travelled, which I haven't; I know you've seen the world, which I haven't, but does that give you the right to say my life's been wasted? I don't believe it does.

He was too stunned to speak.

— Don't interrupt me, she said in the silence. — You think because you write books that you understand other people's hearts and minds. But you don't, believe me you don't. 'Oh, Jessie, you haven't had much of a life,' you said. How the hell – bless my Christian soul – would you know?

He could have replied, but didn't, that Jessie Chapman – as far as he was aware – had been at her mother's demanding beck and call from her schooldays onwards. There had been one prospective lover, but he'd failed to meet with Alice Chapman's approval, and her acidic judgement of his character had meant curtains for Stanley. No romance, no adventure, no real culture – such had been his sister's miserable lot. Or so it seemed on the surface.

— Jessie, I must apologise.

— You don't have to. Just keep your trap shut once in a while.

It was, he conceded, good advice. He was in the literary business of delving beneath surfaces, and here he was judging his sister with the superficiality of a mere gossip. How dare he? How dare he belittle her? He wasn't privy to her deepest feelings, whatever curious form they took. They were hers alone to express or to keep secret. That was the nub of it.

He would often think to himself that Jessie might have had a better time on earth, but he never said so again. When she, too, was dead he remarked to Graham as they left the hospital that he was distressed beyond words for what Alice had done to her hapless daughter.

— You're being dramatic, Harry. Jessie was happy enough. She made few demands on people. And her last illness was mercifully quick. She'd be upset, and not a little angry, if she knew you were sad about her relationship with the remarkable Alice. Jessie coped. There's much to be said in favour of those who cope.

In the late 1940s, Sir William Lilliburn's charity school – its motto was 'Better Deathe than Deceite' – opened its doors to boys who had not been awarded a scholarship to study in its hallowed halls. Harry was the honoured possessor of a bursary, and Leo Duggan's father was rich enough to pay for his son's education, but the likes of Ralph Edmunds and his cronies lacked the academic skills required of generations of Lilliburnians from 1700 onwards. They were good at games, but little else.

Harry Chapman wondered, now, what Leo Duggan, the friend who had introduced him to Mendelssohn and Babar the Elephant, would have thought of his liaison with Leo's tormentor, so cavalier with words of abuse such as 'Yid' and 'kike'.

— The Ralph Edmundses of this world are best ignored. Leave them to stew in their own filthy juice.

He had dined, and attended concerts, with Leo and Eleanor during the years of his Queequeg and Ishmael assignations. Once, the conversation had drifted onto the subject of anti-Semitism in post-war Britain and Leo had remembered the first occasion on which Ralph and his braying followers had pointed to his circumcised cock and joked about the size and shape of his nose – or 'conk', as they called it. Two nights before, Harry had lain with Ralph in a Bloomsbury hotel after being squeezed breathless in the shower.

— Poor brainless Ralph, said the gentle Leo. I hope he made something of himself. He came from a rough background.

— I hope so, too, the secretive Harry Chapman concurred. – I really hope so.

What was this music he was hearing?

— It's a song by Brahms, the sixteen-year-old Leo tells him. — 'Gestillte Sehnsucht', or 'Satisfied Longing'. It's Ma's particular favourite. She becomes very weepy every time she hears it. Once a week, Harry, to be precise.

— And who is that singing?

— You don't know? You poor Babar-starved Harry. That's Kathleen Ferrier, no less. Ma, Pa and I think she has the loveliest voice in the world.

When the song is over, Leo explains its meaning. The unhappy singer, in the golden glow of evening, hears the soft voices of birds and prepares herself for sleep. But this sleep, Leo says with a smile, is obviously the final one – the last sleep that eradicates every pain, every earthly longing, leaving only peace.

— That's morbid, Leo.

— No, it's not. I can't say why, but it's not morbid at all when the music is very beautiful.

Harry Chapman, thinking of the Queequeg and Ishmael of Melville's imagination, recalled his previous stay in hospital, twenty-seven years earlier. He'd had an abscess on his upper gums which his dentist – a cheery New Zealander with permanent bad breath – had been unable and unwilling to remove. The specialist at Roehampton had noticed that he was holding a copy of *Moby-Dick* and had asked him if he was mad.

— Don't misunderstand me, Mr Chapman. By 'mad' I don't mean certifiably insane, I just mean mad enough to read a book as long and rambling as that. It's about a whale, isn't it?

— Partly.

— I like suspense myself.

— You don't have a sufficiency in your work?

— If I answered 'yes', you wouldn't let me perform the operation. There will be no suspense tomorrow, I can promise.

So the madman sat on a bench in the hospital grounds that warm summer afternoon and opened the much-loved book and scanned the familiar pages. There was a 'damp, drizzly November' in his own soul as he attempted, and failed, to read on. He had learned recently of the unexpected death of an actor of his own age whom he'd shared a scene with in a television cops series. Victor had looked the fittest of the fit, treating his body as if it were a temple. And then, on the third of July, 1980, running around his local park with his teenage son keeping pace with him, Victor stopped to take what would be his final breath. He opened his mouth, made to clutch his heart, and fell to earth for ever.

Melville's words swam in front of him. He felt then as he'd felt as a boy, standing in the graveyard of St Mary's Church, reading the names and dates and pious tributes on the blackened tombstones. Those Joshuas, Elizas, Alexanders and Lydias had been a long time mouldering, with generation upon generation of worms taking sustenance from their remains. This was man's fate – a progress from nothing into nothingness.

Later that evening, in the ward, he joined a group of male patients who were watching a television documentary about Laurel and Hardy. Stan Laurel's face reminded him of his father's, and his sense of futility deepened, if that were possible. He smiled, of course, as the incomparable pair tried to carry a piano up a flight of steps, just as he'd smiled as a small boy at the very same sequence in his local cinema, the Super Palace. It was known as a fleapit, and the auditorium always smelled of an especially lethal disinfectant. That smell returned to him briefly as he watched the dead comics, immortalised on celluloid.

The programme ended, and someone switched off the set. The men started talking. A man in his twenties was the immediate focus of their attention. They demanded to hear more stories of his sexual exploits. The blond cockney Lothario, whose right leg was in plaster, was happy to regale his eager audience with the adventures that had brought him to this pretty pass of broken bones and torn ligaments.

Lothario, alias Brian, had jumped from a balcony to avoid a confrontation with an angry husband who had returned to the second-floor flat he shared with his wife, 'an old woman pushing forty'. Brian, hearing a key turning in the front door, had slipped out of Mrs Paterson with greater speed than he had slipped into her, and – clutching his trousers, shirt and underpants – he'd climbed over the railing and leapt to freedom, leaving the naked Mrs P and his second-best pair of moccasins behind. He'd hobbled away from the scene of the crime in only his cotton socks, 'in complete bleeding agony', and got his clothes back on in an alley, and now he was an invalid, thanks to a few minutes of fun and games with a sex-mad ratbag.

Brian had a fiancée, Harry learned, and the lucky girl's lovely mother very much approved of the match. Whenever the daughter was off on her travels – she had a job with a perfume company, with branches outside London – Mummy gave her future son-in-law a thorough workout in the master bedroom.

It was generally agreed among the listeners that his marriage, if it ever happened, would end in tears. Everyone asked for an invitation to the wedding – which had been postponed because of his accident – when it was rescheduled. They would come to the church laden with tons of confetti to throw at the bride, who would be a vision in white, and the groom, in his top hat and tails. If there was any left over, they'd sprinkle Brian's in-laws with it, as a token of respect for the mother in particular, who had managed to keep a straight face throughout the ceremony.

Harry Chapman reckoned that Brian, if he hadn't been murdered by a cuckolded husband or by one of his discarded lovers, would be in his late forties now. He pictured him as a portly raconteur, with hundreds of personal anecdotes at his command, inspiring new and younger Lotharios to feats of recklessness. Perhaps his wife had borne him a son, the identical model of his devious dad, who was leaping off balconies, hiding in wardrobes, sticking on false moustaches and presently re-enacting all the dear, familiar clichés of theatrical adultery, while Harry – no longer subscribing to the idea of the futility of human existence – clung on to his life, what little there was left of it, in the Zoffany Ward.

Young Harry Chapman was alone in the Chapmans' half of the house that afternoon. He turned on the radio, or the 'wireless' as everybody called it in those days, and was soon compelled to listen intently. A man was describing the progress of a tennis match, and Harry had to make sense of unfamiliar words such as 'forehand', 'backhand', 'volley' and 'lob'. 'Love', which up till now he had associated with affection, suddenly meant 'nothing' or 'nothing on the scoreboard'. Harry had never seen anyone play tennis, because there were no courts at school. Football and cricket were the games on the curriculum, and Harry hated both, especially the latter. The boys in his class had laughed at him when he'd gone in to bat, closing his eyes in fear as the hard ball was bowled in his direction. He was declared to be a coward at the wicket, and was happy to be relegated to the rank of bored spectator.

He was intrigued by what he was hearing. One of the players, Jaroslav Drobny, a Czech who claimed Egyptian nationality, seemed to be the crowd's favourite, judging by the loud applause that greeted every winning shot. His opponent, an American with the very American name Budge Patty, was making it a fierce, closely fought contest.

For years afterwards, whenever he attended the championships at Wimbledon, Harry Chapman would marvel that he had been bewitched by tennis long before he had ever seen a ball served and put into play. He saw himself, now, in the poky kitchen, his ears attuned to Max Robertson's vivid commentary, deciding on the instant that if there was a single sport in the world he might possibly enjoy it could only be tennis.

The pain in his gut returned with renewed force.

— Oh, God. Oh, dear God.

Nancy Driver was soon at his side.

— Harry? What's up, my sweet?

— It's back. I'd hoped it had gone away, but no such luck.

— I'll see if I can find Dr Pereira.

— Please. Please.

Jack, the ever-present, ever-reliable ship-boy, advised him to be calm. Harry had no cause to panic.

No, perhaps not. Perhaps this was, at last, the end. So be it, he thought, while wishing it were otherwise. So bloody be it.

— At least you're in a clean hospital bed, son, not in a stinking filthy, Flanders trench like me.

— Yes, Dad.

— With the rats coming out at night to see if I'm fodder yet.

— Yes, Dad, I'm lucky.

He was aware that Dr Pereira was looking down at him.

— Harry, I need to put a little pressure on your stomach. I'll be as gentle as possible.

Gentle as the doctor was, he wasn't gentle enough for Harry Chapman, who cried out in agony.

— I'm going to give you a sedative, Harry. I want to make the next few hours easy for you.

Ah, the magic potion again, administered by the curly-haired fruitseller, in his white hospital coat.

— There, Harry. I'll be back tomorrow morning. You'll be able to rest now.

— Harry Chapman, I'm not going to call you a third time. If you don't get out of bed this instant, you'll be late for school.

What was the point of leaving the warmth of the blankets and sheets for the chill of a December morning? His father, who had slept alongside him for the last six months, was dead and only recently buried and the pointlessness of rising, washing and dressing for a new day was uppermost in his eleven-year-old mind. Yet rise he did, at the behest of his sister Jessie, when she admonished him gently for not respecting their daddy's memory.

— He wanted you to have the education he never had.

This was a truth he could neither ignore nor deny. He studied French – the inexplicable language Frank called 'parlee-vous' – with special application that Wednesday. He would bring honour to the Chapman name, he thought as he mastered the present tense of the verbs *être* and *avoir*. He would make that his mission in life.

— Education's all very well, but too much of it can bring you trouble, said his mother, dispensing the wisdom she imparted to him throughout his schooldays and beyond.

He shrugged by way of reply.

— You'll mark the truth of my words one day.

— Leave the boy be, Alice.

— You always take his side, Rosy Glow.

She takes everyone's side, the young Harry Chapman heard his older self explain to the dead woman who had brought him into being, because she understands what few of us are granted to understand – that we all merit, whatever our failings, some acknowledgement of our worth. Aunt Rose had acknowledged her nephew's worthiness from his infancy.

— You lovely boy.

He had been 'lovely' for once or twice in the year, when Rose had come to visit. Jessie had been designated 'lovely', too. Aunt Rose had brought them fruit and sweets and chocolates and little pictures of St Francis of Assisi, who, she said, for all that he was a Catholic, was someone in touch with birds and animals and plants and the wonders of the universe. He was her hero of heroes, and she'd happened upon him by chance, through nursing a dying Jesuit, back in her early days of tending the sick.

— You were a nurse, Auntie Rose?

— Of course I was, forgetful Harry.

Yes, yes, he remembered, now, his sweet-natured aunt had cared for the elderly at a home in the seaside town Broadstairs. She had gone there in her late twenties and remained *in situ* until she was sixty, when she decided to live 'like a lady of leisure' on her pension. So the kind soul who would end her days in the Eventide Home, talking to the mischievous, invisible Gertie, had cared for hundreds of people who had their own unseen friends and acquaintances.

How many funerals can a man have? And just how many times can he die?

These were the questions nagging Harry Chapman as he lay in an open coffin waiting for the service to begin. There wasn't even a hint of gold, which led him to believe that this repeat performance was taking place in somewhere other than St Mark's.

— Hello and goodbye, said a grinning Christopher. — I'm here to make sure you've gone.

— Very kind of you. As thoughtful as ever.

— It was the least I could do.

Then it was Wilfred Granger's turn to pay his last respects.

— I wish I had your luck, Harry. I may look healthy, but I'm really very ill. First of all, my heart. Second, my diabetes. Third, my prostate. Fourth, my ingrowing toenail. And you never had to endure cataracts, did you?

— I'm so sorry for you, Wilf.

— I wish other people were. It's a cruel, uncaring world we live in. Oh, the indignity of getting old.

An exasperated Alice Chapman had no sympathy for the whining individual who was saying goodbye to her son.

— Push off, misery guts. What kind of man are you? Moan, moan, moan. Is that what Harry wants to hear at a time like this? No, it bloody well isn't.

Actually, it bloody well was what he wanted to hear because Wilf's limitless self-concern and self-pity amused Harry Chapman. He couldn't explain to his mother – who was no longer there, anyhow – why this was so. She had always found his sense of humour peculiar.

The NIL BY MOUTH sign was in place once more.

— How's the pain, Harry?

— It seems to have gone away for the moment. Is that you, Marybeth?

— One and the same.

— Is it morning, afternoon or evening?

— The latter.

— I shan't be leaving here this week, shall I?

— That's not for me to say. Try not to worry about it too much. I know that's easier said than done, but try, honey.

'Honey' would try his best to be stoical. He managed to mutter Edgar's wonderful – to Harry Chapman wonderful – lines in *King Lear*:

— *The worst is not,*
So long as we can say 'This is the worst.'

— That bears a lot to think about and mull over, said Marybeth Myslawchuk, blowing him a kiss as she left him alone in his bed near the main entrance to, and exit from, the Zoffany Ward.

Tuesday – Wednesday –
Thursday – Friday

— THERE ISN'T MUCH to shave down here, Mr Chapman, said Maciek Nazwisko. — Just a few days' growth.

— Can you count the hairs?

— Four and a half. The half is just a tiny – how you say? – sprout.

— In five days? That's a miracle.

Where had he read, in his youth, that human hair and nails have an independent life? You die, and if you're not cremated but buried, the hairs on your head, if you're not totally bald, and your body, if you are hirsute, and the nails on your fingers and toes keep growing while the rest of you rots.

— You're ready for theatre now, Mr Chapman.

— Thank you, Maciek.

He was placed on a gurney and taken along the same corridors and wheeled into the same capacious lift which plunged downwards. A new someone commented on his paleness to a new another, who responded that she'd seen more colour in an uncooked fillet of cod.

If I ever get out of here, I shall use that remark one day, the novelist in him thought.

— We meet again, said Dr Helen Burgess, the anaesthetist. — You know the procedure.

— Yes.

She examined him thoroughly, and told him she still felt confident to go ahead.

He heard her wish him good luck before the anaesthetic took Harry Chapman away from every sight and sound.

These men were doctors — that much was clear — because they had stethoscopes draped down their white coats. One of them was saying:

— Gentlemen, what we have here is a most interesting specimen. This human object we are examining has eaten nothing but peas for the past three months. Fresh garden peas, tinned peas, frozen peas, and haricot beans for variation. Observe the effects, gentlemen. Examine him, examine him, if you please. If the body emits natural gas, then the peas have served our purpose. The patient's pulse is irregular, is it not?

— It is, Doctor, says a lone voice.

— And his eyes, see how dead they are. They lack all lustre, gentlemen. It must be our immediate purpose to restore their sparkle. How do we achieve that end?

— No more peas, Doctor. Change his diet.

— Excellent thinking. Let us move to the next bed, gentlemen, where we will find another fascinating case. What we have here is a throwback to the beasts of the field. That is why he is kept in chains. He has been fed nothing but dried bread and water for six months. Approach him at your peril, gentlemen.

— Harry?

— Is that you, Dad?

— Who else could it be, my son? What are you doing

here with me? How the hell did you get through the German lines?

— I followed my nose, I suppose, the very young Harry Chapman replied, and giggled. — I'm a poet who doesn't know it.

— Listen, Harry boy, this is no place for you. If I die at the hands of the Hun, you stand no chance of ever being born. Go back to your mother, whoever she is.

— Her name's Alice.

— Alice Bartrip? So I marry Alice, the pretty girl with the sharp tongue, do I? Well, well, wonders will never cease. Her sister Rose has a kinder nature, but it's Alice who gives me wet dreams. Don't you dare tell her I said that.

It was good to be with his father again. They had been apart for sixty years. Frank looked like the shy young man in uniform in the sepia photograph Jessie had discovered in Alice's 'secret drawer' after their mother's death. And Harry, of course, couldn't see himself, but he could hear his own treble, childish voice, burbling happily against the steady noise of guns and bombs.

— Now you're here, you'd best make yourself comfortable. Keep your head down for Christ's sake, Harry. We don't want you connecting with a stray bullet.

He sat down in the dark, damp trench. Frank's fellow soldiers were no more than shadows.

Then the sky turned red and white by turns, and the frightened little boy huddled in the warmth and safety of his daddy's arms.

This was music of a kind new to his ears. It was like nothing he had heard before and had never anticipated hearing.

— This is my country, said Antal, Harry's friend of an hour. — This is the soul of my country.

Harry listened, even as he revelled in Antal's beauty.

— He, too, was in exile at the end. As I am now, pretty Harry. I can't believe I shall ever see Budapest again.

It was the summer of 1959. Three years earlier, there had been a failed uprising in Hungary. Soviet tanks had stormed through the capital. Antal's father – Antal told his very new friend – had faced a firing squad. You don't face a firing squad and live.

Antal poured more whisky into Harry's slightly chipped glass.

— You care for my beloved Bartók, Harry?

— Yes, I do. I do very much.

— He is, as I say, our soul.

Harry had heard *Mikrokosmos* hundreds of times since that June evening in Antal's furnished room in a house near Knightsbridge, and on each occasion the face of the Hungarian actor had appeared to him just as he'd seen it when Antal told him the pianist was Geza Anda, a name that would stay in his memory.

— Geza Anda was born to play Bartók, Harry.

What an educative sexual encounter that turned out to be. Harry had not expected to discover a composer or to learn of a family's tragic fate when he stopped to look in a shop window in order to speak to the man who was following him. Their eyes had met, they'd smiled, and Harry had accepted the stranger's offer to go back for a coffee.

In March that year, Harry had played his first and last substantial role on the professional stage, as a cockney waif in a verse play by Marigold Jeavons. It was called *The Game of Chance* and no one in the cast of six understood what it was about. It was a ritualistic piece, with everyone speaking in unison at key moments in the drama. The audiences throughout the two-week run had either cheered or booed at the final curtain, and Harry and the other five members of the East End gang had assumed stoical expressions as their supporters and denigrators turned the auditorium into a battlefield. Only Marigold was delighted with the response, likening it to that which greeted the first performance of Stravinsky's *The Rite of Spring*, or *Le Sacre du printemps*, as she unfailingly referred to it. 'It's my *Sacre*,' she would tell her 'brave darling ones', adding 'and yours too, my loves'.

— I did not see it, Harry.

— Thank God you didn't, Antal. I wouldn't be lying here with you if you'd witnessed me playing the fool for over two hours.

Antal continued acting long after his lover of three blissful months became a novelist. He never lost his thick, beguiling accent, which he used to sinister effect in a number of horror movies. Harry liked to think that when Antal plunged a stake through an evil Russian colonel's heart, he had – perhaps – his own father's murder in mind.

— God did a good day's work when He invented the sardine, said Alice Chapman as she opened the tin with her customary dexterity.

Oh, those tins, and the keys that came with them. Harry was all fingers and thumbs, and then more fingers and thumbs, whenever he had to manipulate the hated key, which always refused to function for him. It would get halfway across the lid and stop and remain immovable.

— The stupid bloody thing.

— Are you talking about yourself?

— No, I'm not, Mother, and you know it.

— I know that you're useless with your hands. And I don't know why you are. Your father was the best handyman in the world.

— Well, I'm not, and I never will be, as you are thrilled to remind your hopeless son.

She cut off a large knob of butter and mashed the sardines into it. Within minutes, she had made a delicious paste to spread on toast. This was one of his favourite meals, and he could savour it now, wherever he was.

Wherever he was, it wasn't the kitchen in the house near the gasworks and the candle factory. It was a brighter, sunnier place, with high ceilings and as much space as he had ever craved. He munched his sardine-butter toast until a youthful waiter guided him to a table by the window.

The waiter opened a folded napkin with a flourish after he had seen Harry Chapman sitting comfortably in an expansive chair.

There was no menu to be consulted. The chef knew exactly what Signor Chapman wanted to eat, as well as the wines he favoured.

— *Buon appetito.*

And so the feast began. He looked about him to see if there were any other diners – but no, he was alone; he was splendidly alone. Yes, he sat in splendour while the exquisite food was set before him – soup and fish as a prelude, then lamb done in the Roman style, then calf's liver, then roast beef with Yorkshire pudding, then pheasant and partridge and venison. The white wine was a Pinot from Friuli and the red a rich Barolo. Cheeses came next – Taleggio, accompanied by a ripe pear; Stilton, with a glass of port; and a hunk of mature Cheddar, resting in state beside a tantalising dollop of chutney. A chocolate mousse, flavoured subtly with a hint of rosemary, was brought to the hungry guest, who licked his spoon when the bowl was empty.

Why, after this surfeit of food, these dishes of a lifetime, was Harry Chapman still famished? His stomach was growling. He should have felt bloated, incapable of movement, but he clicked his fingers and when the waiter reappeared, an old man now instead of the youth who had welcomed him – he had aged almost imperceptibly with each course while the meal was in progress – the solitary diner asked if he could go back to the soup and fish and eat everything, every single delicious thing, all over again. The waiter shed fifty years and bowed.

It was with the arrival of the venison, surrounded by juniper berries, that the newly ancient waiter collapsed and died in the room that was neither bright nor sunny. Harry Chapman, starved of sustenance, banged his knife and fork on the table and wept in frustration that this basic need was being denied him.

— Here's God's best invention, Harry. Fill your face with toast and sardine butter, my son.

— Harry.
— Is that you? Is that you, Graham?
— It is.

— Who is this Graham person, Harry?
— He's the dear, kind man I live with. You'd been dead four years when I met him.
— I hope, for your sake, he's sensible.
— He is.
— He needs to be, with a dreamer like you. If Harry Chapman's feet were ever on the ground, I can't say as how I noticed.

Hadn't she noticed that her son wished to escape from the refined but desperate poverty into which he was born? Hadn't she heard him lament that there has to be something more beautiful to contemplate than the view of the gasworks and the candle factory? Obviously not, for if she had she would have understood why he was a dreamer. That was why his feet, itching to be gone, were seldom on the ground.

— That Christopher was sensible until he went mad.

— I think you can say that about a lot of people, Mother.

— Do you still see him?

— I try not to, but he finds a way of inveigling –

— 'In' what?

— He finds a way of contacting me, even though he's dead. As you do.

— I only have your welfare in mind.

— Thank you. Can I ask you a question?

— You can, for all the good it will do you.

— Did you really work for Virginia and Leonard Woolf?

There was no immediate reply. He waited for her to speak. He was on the point of saying that of course she didn't when Alice Chapman, cackling to herself, answered:

— That would be telling, wouldn't it? Those two were worse than royalty in regard to confidences. They were frightened we'd spill the beans, us mongrels, about their funny habits.

— So you *did* work for them?

— As I say, that would be telling, wouldn't it?

Here we go round Alice Chapman's ever-blossoming mulberry bush, he thought. She loved her riddles, her teasing little games with her children, her husband, and the world at large. They added a touch of mystery to her humdrum everyday life.

— Oh, Mother, you could tell me now.

— I could, if I had a mind to. But perhaps I haven't.

He took a sudden vow of silence. Why should he waste precious words? The Trappists know that silence is the virtue of virtues, and the time had come to emulate them, as he had failed to do in the past.

— Aren't you going to say anything?

He was tempted to answer no, but this was one temptation he was pleased to resist.

— This must be the first time the cat has got your tongue.

Was it? He'd been monkish in the face of Christopher's insults, to his tormenting lover's annoyance. The proverbial cat had captured and eaten his tongue on those terrible nights.

— I haven't upset you, have I?

No, she hadn't upset him. But was he upsetting her, by refusing to respond? He surprised himself by hoping he wasn't. Harry, the Trappist he ought to have been, wanted nothing but peace between them.

— I know, I know to my cost, Harry, what differences we've had, but can't you just say a kind word back to me?

One kind word would lead to another, and another, and no kind word in the dictionary would be kind enough to placate the unassuageable soul of Alice Chapman.

— You can kill with kindness, Prince Myshkin (entrapped in permanent isolation) reminded his friend Harry.

He heeded the Prince's wise caution without acknowledging it. His mother, her ears cocked for every utterance, would assume he was addressing her.

— He prefers not to speak to you, pronounced Bartleby, coming to Harry's rescue, and that seemed to settle the matter, for Alice left in a huff, slamming decades of doors behind her. This was the huff of all huffs, outhuffing – if there was such a term – the huffs she had created, engineered, manoeuvred, fallen victim to, in the years of her marriage and motherhood.

Now that she had vanished, Harry Chapman felt the need to speak to her.

— Graham?
— I'm here.

Wasn't it agreed, on God only knows what scant evidence, that when you are dying, your whole life flashes before you? Your *whole* life? Well, the Grim Reaper wasn't ready for him yet, because nothing like his whole life – with those innumerable moments of boredom; those days of blank despair – was in his sights.

— Harry?
— Aunt Rose. Oh, it's lovely to see you.
— Likewise, as those Yanks say.

It was Harry and Jessie's first Christmas without their father, and here was their aunt bringing tidings of comfort and great joy to the bereaved family. Dear Frank, she told her unhappy and angry sister, would want everyone to be as happy as possible, under the circumstances.

— You can make yourself useful, Rose, by getting out of my kitchen. I'll allow you to lay the table, and then you can park your fanny in the one comfortable armchair.
— Must you be so vulgar, Alice?
— If I'm being vulgar, why are you smiling?
— Because I just heard the old Alice, the Alice I grew up with. The sister with the fighting spirit.

That there was love between Malice and Rosy Glow, demonstrated in frowns as much as smiles, their son and nephew did not doubt.

Perhaps Rose envied her sibling's gift of acerbity, and perhaps Alice sometimes thought that her own path through life might have been less bumpy if she hadn't judged others so harshly, Harry, the consummate supposer – if there was such a term – supposed.

— Roast chicken, Alice? What a wonderful surprise.

— The children expect it. I cook chicken on their birthdays and at Easter and Christmas. It's our family luxury.

She stifled a sob on the word 'luxury'.

— Oh, Alice, my dear –

— Frank always made the same awful joke, year after year. 'Not chicken again, woman,' he'd say. And I'd pretend to be cross with him.

Jessie looked at her brother, who smiled back.

There were four sixpenny pieces hidden in the Christmas pudding, and by some miracle Jessie found two in her portion and Harry two in his.

— I shall know where to come if I ever need to borrow money, said Aunt Rose, beaming at her niece and nephew.

— I haven't gone away.

It was the rarest of summer afternoons. The sky was unclouded and the heat was bearable.

Harry Chapman was at his happiest. He had written well that morning, and now here he was in the stands at Wimbledon waiting for the men's singles final to begin.

On to the court came the reigning champion, Roger Federer, but alongside him was a player from a different, bygone age. Who could it be? The man wore glasses and seemed to have none of the physical grace of his elegant rival.

— Mr Drobny has elected to serve, the umpire informed the excited crowd.

Mr Drobny? Was Harry going to see the phantom at last? The heroic Jaroslav, the Czech out of Egypt who had once lived in England, was about to challenge the young conqueror, the possessor already of ten Grand Slam titles.

— Federer leads by four games to one.

Harry Chapman was now relying on the umpire for news of the match's progress, because the sunlight of early July was blinding him. No matter how much he squinted or blinked, he could see nothing but an unending whiteness.

— Mr Laver leads by five games to two in the final set.

Ah, that respectful 'Mister'. That's how it used to be in the gentlemanly olden days.

He waited, in anticipation, for the next umpirical – was there such a word? – pronouncement.

— Federer leads Mr Tilden by two sets to one.

Yes, yes – it would have been 'Mr Tilden', then. Nowadays the Ladies, God bless them, are still addressed as 'Miss' or 'Mrs' at Wimbledon. 'Ms' has yet to be heard on those hallowed courts.

— Six all. Tie break.

But who was playing whom?

— *Égalité*.

Why was the umpire suddenly reverting to French?

— *Avantage, Mademoiselle Lenglen*.

No, this couldn't be. This simply couldn't be.

— *Jeu*.

Someone was being applauded, but he couldn't determine who it was. Voices were saying that this was championship point.

— Deuce.

A collective groan, expressing concern and frustration, echoed round the Centre Court. Harry Chapman made his own feeble contribution to it.

— Advantage, Rosewall.

What on earth was going on? Rosewall, Federer's equal in elegance, had retired in the 1970s. He had been Harry Chapman's hero then, as Federer was now.

— Racket abuse. Second caution, Mr McEnroe.

— You can not be serious, shrieked the furious contestant.

— I was never more serious in my life. I swear on my mother's immortal soul that I am as serious as I shall ever be. I am the very epitome of seriousness. But wait a moment – did you say 'serious' or 'Sirius'? If the latter, I have to inform you that, yes, I can not be Sirius, since Sirius is the brightest star in the sky after the sun, lying in the constellation Canis Major. For your additional edification, I can also inform you that Sirius is a binary star whose companion, Sirius B, is a very faint white dwarf. Sirius is known, variously, as the Dog Star, Canicula and Sothis. Ergo: I am serious, but I can not be Sirius. Shall we continue with the match? Resume play, if you please. Federer to serve.

He was standing with Graham in the Accademia in Florence. They were looking at Michelangelo's statue of David when Graham began to laugh.

— What's so funny?

— It's that hand on his hip. You'd think he was cruising Goliath. I can just hear him saying 'Come on, big boy. Have you got a special something for me?' I'm sorry, Harry. I'm a heretic.

As they walked towards the Ponte Vecchio, Harry remembered being a silent worshipper in May 1949 in the public baths with the swimming pool that reeked of chlorine. That other David, Cooke by name, was still there in his mind, striking the same nonchalant pose as he'd done that day when the pigeon-chested Harry emerged from the water he had yellowed blinded by sun and glass.

— I like the notion of Goliath being rough trade.

— None rougher, Harry. Ask David. He reckons Golly, as he calls him, is an absolutely gorgeous brute.

— Graham?

— He's answering a call of nature, Mr Chapman, said a nurse he didn't recognise. — He'll be back very soon.

— Where's that gushing nurse? And the bullet-headed doctor who calls his patients 'Sunshine'?

— Nurse Dunckley has left us. Mr Russell, if that's who you mean, has been taken ill. I am Evelina, by the way. I am from Finland, before you ask.

— What time of day is it?

— Eight thirty on Wednesday evening.

— Thank you, Evelina.

— I hope and pray that this Graham person, whoever he is, isn't taking advantage of you.

— Taking advantage? What do you mean, Mother?

— You're such a child where people are concerned. You let them tread all over you. You've never been cautious enough.

— Cautious?

— Yes. They say nice things to you and you believe them. I've watched you being taken in. Harry, you're as daft as silly old Rosy Glow at times. She sees the sunshine where she ought to see the rain, and you are just as blind as she is.

— Am I?

— Yes, my boy, you are. I worry about you, I honestly do. Life isn't a book, though I bet you wish it was.

He needed to tell her, now, that some of the books he loved were full of disturbance and chaos and unresolved dilemmas – quite like life, in fact – but the words wouldn't come to him.

— Mother, he remarked instead, — it was your resistance that inspired me to write. Let me continue, uninterrupted. I've always wanted to do fictional justice to people who aren't cultivated. So many novels are concerned with rarefied creatures, blessed or cursed with high intelligence, but my concern was, and is, with the Franks and Alices and Jessies and Roses, the ones who are seldom honoured with beautiful sentences and paragraphs. You challenged me to love you with your endless gibes and you turned me, superficially, into a parody of your cynical self. You gave me the worst of you, but I was determined to dig and dig, archaeologically, until I chanced upon the best in you, the best you buried. And I found it, Mother, in the book I wrote after your death. I care to think I granted you a few beautiful sentences at least.

There, he had told her. Would she respond to his heartfelt outpouring with a ready sarcasm? He would soon find out.

— I don't know much about beautiful sentences, whatever they are. And I can't say as how I follow your drift, Harry. But there's none of your usual mockery in your voice.

He refrained from saying there was none in hers, either.

— Harry, my son, whispered Frank, suddenly appearing at his wife's side. — It's good to see and hear the pair of you going easy on each other. I'd hoped you'd grow up to be a stranger to moodiness, but my hope was dashed a bit, wasn't it?

'A stranger to moodiness' – there was that phrase again, on the lips of his laconic father, Private 36319 Chapman, survivor of the horrors of Passchendaele, which was Passion Dale to his young son's ears.

Moodiness, garbed in red and black, had visited Harry Chapman in that desolate time that began with Frank's burial.

— Hello there, Harry Chapman. I'm Moodiness.

— Hello.

— I've been a friend of your mother for many a long year.

— You don't need to remind me.

— So shall we strike up an acquaintance?

— Why not?

— Just for the hell of it.

— Exactly.

— That's the spirit, Harry.

Harry Chapman looked on as Frank and Alice embraced, in the way they must have done before he was born. He couldn't recall their being this affectionate during his childhood. Such a display of mutual tenderness might have happened in private, once their children were in bed and soundly asleep, but nowhere else. Harry smiled that he was audience, at last, to Frank's love for Alice, and Alice's for Frank.

— Don't go any further, Alice cautioned her eager husband. — A certain little nosy parker has his eye on us.

— Get along with you, son. Your mother and myself have some unfinished business to attend to.

— Have you answered your call of nature?

— Yes, Harry. Thank you for asking.

— My mind's all over the place.

— Not to worry.

— Is it still Wednesday?

— Just about.

— Will there be chimes at midnight? What a silly question.

— It's a very silly question.

The youthful waiter led him to the same table by the same window in the same bright and sunlit room.

He sat in the same capacious chair. There was a place card on the white tablecloth in the name of Lucius Licinius Lucullus.

Harry Chapman was about to observe that the restaurateur had made a mistake when he remembered that Lucullus was a wealthy Roman famous for his lavish banquets. The card was a joke, a prank, to amuse the honoured guest.

The meal began with *antipasti*: artichokes; Parma ham; dried beef from Lombardy; and a salad of fennel and cucumber.

When the waiter arrived with the fish courses, he had aged by a decade. That was Harry Chapman's supposition.

There were langoustines, clams, seared tuna, fried scampi and calamari, sardines and lobster fritters for Harry to enjoy.

What a feast, he remarked to the waiter, whose hair was now greying at the temples.

At Easter, he ate roast suckling lamb, to the accompaniment of church bells, and then – as the leaves turned vivid red and golden brown on the trees – a whole pheasant was set before him. The bird was of an astonishing sweetness, having been marinated in milk and Muscat wine. The waiter was stooping slightly when he returned to take the plates away.

He was bent over the next time he came into view.

— Would His Excellency care for a lemon sorbet to clean his palate?

— That's a lovely idea. Would you be kind enough to pour a measure of vodka over it?

— Your wish is my command.

The waiter was supporting himself with a stick now.

— You don't look very well, said a concerned Harry Chapman.

— Duty is duty, sire.

In what seemed like hours later, the old man's duties were fulfilled. He had lost all his teeth and most of his white hair. He sank to his knees with the words:

— Mine has been a lifetime of service. Let me go to my rest.

The famished Harry Chapman, alias Lucius Licinius Lucullus, cast his greed and selfishness aside and took the dying waiter in his arms.

— You deserve your rest, if anyone does.

— I still want you to tell me, loud and clear, that this Graham person, whoever he is, isn't taking advantage of you.

— He isn't, Mother. It's the other way round. It's me who is taking advantage of him.

— How's that?

— This is how. He is the ideal companion. Ours is a marriage of curious minds. When we first met, three years after Christopher found lasting refuge from his foul temper, Graham was mourning the loss of a loved one. Early on in our relationship we dispensed with something I have never talked to you about. You once described it as 'what goes on down there'. Well, we tried 'what goes on down there' and it didn't really work and 'what goes on down there' quickly became 'what went on down there' and we laughed it out of our thoughts.

— I wish I could believe you.

— Try to.

— Yes, Alice, believe what your son is telling you, Aunt Rose intervened.

— Believe him, Mum, Jessie pleaded.

— I'll give it a try, Alice Chapman said quietly. — That's all I can promise to do.

*   *   *

— *Aimez-vous Brahms?* an unexpectedly cheerful, even hysterical Christopher was asking him.

— *Oui*.

— I don't. I never did. And would you believe it – I've made two friends, two very distinguished friends, who hate his music, too.

— I think I know who they are. Hugo Wolf, perhaps? And Benjamin Britten? Yes, Christopher?

— Yes, yes, you shit.

Harry Chapman, picturing Christopher with his chums Hugo and Ben, hummed the opening bars of the Second Piano Concerto just to annoy the three of them.

— Is it Thursday yet?

— Yes, Mr Chapman, it is, replied Veronica.

— Veronica?

— That's me.

— Where am I?

— You're back in Zoffany. You were moved overnight.

— Where's Graham?

— He's gone home to grab some sleep. Sister Driver and Marybeth and Philip will be on duty soon.

— That's good, he said. — That *is* good news.

— Be careful, Master Harry, warned Jack the ship-boy as Mr Chapman entered the lecture room in whichever university he was visiting. He had been invited to address the Creative Writing students, and was distressed to see that there were at least a hundred of them. How could a hundred seemingly sane men and women be so naive, so foolish? Why weren't they studying biology, chemistry, history, foreign languages? Why weren't they living their lives to the full? Why the hell were they here?

He began by saying that he wasn't a writer by choice but by vocation. His career, such as it was, dated from early childhood, when he listened to the adults around him and tried to make sense of what they were saying. He was intrigued by the fact that they made hardly any sense at all, for their talk was composed of riddles and secrets and words and phrases that constituted a private language. He listened, where other children might have shut their ears to the chatter going on and on above and about them.

Their prattle refused to yield its secrets, and so – when he had learned to read and write – he turned to books, those depositories of unravelled mysteries, of mysteries acknowledged. He read comics, as every child did, but when he was twelve he embarked on a voyage of discovery that could only end with his death. He read voraciously, then judiciously, and found his writing voice by rejecting the voices of those he was tempted to impersonate.

— So far so calm, Jack murmured in his inner ear.

And what a multitude of friends and acquaintances he'd accumulated – Philip Pirrip, Elizabeth Bennet, Mr Collins, Emma Woodhouse, Don Quixote, Emma Bovary, Jane Eyre, Wilkins Micawber, Hamlet, Rosalind and Orlando, Ishmael and Queequeg –

— Talk about a small world, Skinny Boy –

As well as Prince Myshkin, Jim Hawkins, Long John Silver, and Bartleby, the scrivener, beyond consoling –

— I would prefer that you refrained from mentioning me.

And Dorothea Brooke, Cathy and Heathcliff, and Paolo and Francesca –

— Love brought us to our death, Harry.

It occurred to him that these names, these beloved and familiar names, were not known to the students amassed before him.

The next five minutes were hell for Harry Chapman, despite Jack's efforts to placate him. One girl identified Philip Pirrip as Pip; three were aware of Elizabeth Bennet's enduring fictional existence; no one had an idea who Don Quixote, Emma Bovary and Mr Micawber were, while six – or perhaps it was seven – thought that Hamlet was the guy in Shakespeare who had problems making up his mind. Nobody came to the rescue of Jim Hawkins, and as for Myshkin and Bartleby and Rosalind and Orlando and Paolo and Francesca –

— Love brought us to our death, Harry.

He had to be reasonable. It was too much to expect of them to have any knowledge of Myshkin and Bartleby. But the others, the others. Why hadn't they heard of them?

Shakespeare's ship-boy, Harry's Jack, advised Master Harry to be as tranquil as he could. There were worse problems a man might face, such as guiding a ship out of treacherous waters.

— You cannot write well unless you have read well. If you read trash, God help you, trash will be the result of your labours, if labours they are.

He had nothing more to say. He consulted his watch. He had been booked for another hour.

— Do you have any questions or observations?

Silence ensued.

— Tell me what ideas you have. For your writing, that is.

— I am working on something profound.

— Go on.

— It's set in an unknown country in an unknown period.

— Why?

— That's the way it is.

— Does this profound work have anything as specific, as concrete, as a title?

— Yes. It's called *Hearthrug of Ug*.

Harry stared at the middle-aged man, who was dressed in a dark suit, as if prepared for a day at the office. He wore a stiff white shirt and an undemonstrative tie.

— Does it have characters, your *Hearthrug of Ug*? Do they sit around the hearth, on the rug that I assume belongs to Ug?

— Ug is not a person. It is a philosophical concept.

— Ug is?

— Ug is definitely, definitively, a means of uniting all the philosophies of the world. There can only ultimately be one Ug.

— But why does Ug have need of a hearthrug?

— I don't wish to be rude, Mr Chapman, but are you stupid? Are you, for fuck's sake, fucking stupid?

Those in the class who had been tittering were now gasping in disbelief. Their soberly attired resident lunatic was revealing his manic depths, and in language Harry Chapman might have expected from the younger, wilder, drug-fuelled boys and girls with whom he was trying to communicate.

— I apologise for my stupidity, Mr –

— Ug. I belong to the great brotherhood of Ug. I am Ug in the everlasting order of Ugs.

— Well, then, Mr Ug –

— No 'Mister', Mr Stupid Mr Harry Mr Chapman. There are no 'Misters' in our order of Ugness. We are Ugs, full fucking stop.

Harry Chapman, with all his faults, had never felt the desire to murder. He felt it now. He felt it with a ferocity that was delicious to him. Decapitation, strangulation, a sharp knife to the heart or the gut – oh, the joy of dispatching this smug originator of Ug and Ugness.

— Does anyone else have a question for me?

Silence, again.

To fill that silence, to prevent at whatever cost any further invocation of Ug and the inexplicable hearthrug that was in its possession, Harry Chapman stated that no one could possibly teach another person to write imaginatively. If you have no powers of observation and no insight into character and no flair for language, you cannot expect to be taught them. These were expectations that could never be realised with the assistance of even the most accomplished, dedicated and sympathetic tutor.

In the ten minutes left to him, he told the sad story of the writing life of Herman Melville. He wrote some wonderful short books before producing his masterpiece, *Moby-Dick*. Everything he had written went out of print. For the last nineteen years of his life, he toiled in the New York Customs House, his novels forgotten and ignored. He died in 1891, an irascible and unhappy man. Then, in the 1920s, *Moby-Dick* was rediscovered along with his other writings and since then he has been recognised for what he is – a novelist of genius, a visionary, a writer whose finest prose is of a transcendental beauty. This recognition was denied him while he lived.

The students applauded him when he finished speaking. Even Ug saw fit to clap.

At a reception afterwards, a young woman came up to talk to the distinguished guest. She had a problem, what you might call a dilemma. She felt a real, vital urge to write creatively, but was undecided if the project – Harry Chapman winced at the word – should be a long novel, a collection of short stories, a volume of poetry or a three-act play. What could he suggest?

While he was looking at her, wondering what to say, she suddenly sprouted horns. She was not alone, for everyone present had become a demon.

Why, this was Hell, nor was he out of it.

— Welcome back, Harry, said Nancy Driver. — We're going to give you something nice to eat tonight. Fish, since it's Friday.

He smiled, recalling the two gargantuan meals he had consumed in the bright, sunlit restaurant.

— I hope I have an appetite, Nancy.

— It will only be a small portion.

Was this going to be his third funeral? The guests, or mourners, or visitors, were dressed for an important occasion. He realised, now, that he was standing alone on a stage, in the pleasing glare of a spotlight, while they were taking their seats in the auditorium. Nancy Driver, Marybeth Myslawchuk, Philip Warren, Maciek Nazwisko, Veronica and Dr Pereira were in the front row, alongside Alice, Frank and Jessie Chapman and Aunt Rose, who was glowing as rosily as ever. He could make out, behind them, Leo and Eleanor Duggan, Ralph Edmunds and his sister Beryl, Randolph Breeze and Blanche Westermere, Prince Myshkin, Pip, Emma Woodhouse, Antal, Bartleby and a disgruntled Virginia Woolf. Jeoffrey and Puss, sleek creatures, were being stroked by Pamela, who had turned her back on Wilf Granger. And, dear God, there was Christopher, but without Hugo and Ben.

His performance was about to begin when the Duchess of Bombay, begging pardon upon pardon for her lateness, found a place on the aisle. She was wearing a black T-shirt on which was printed, in bold white letters, the message ANTON VON WEBERN ROCKS.

He was there to recite every single poem he had committed to memory. Soon he was speaking the timeless lines of Shakespeare, Herbert, Milton, Marvell, Anon, Keats, Blake, Smart, Hikmet, Ungaretti, Auden, Eliot and – oh, naughty, naughty Harry – John Wilmot, Earl of Rochester, enjoying the wickedest of rambles in St James's Park. Jack was high above the glare, willing his friend to remember all the words.

On and on went his recital, line after line, century after century. As the hours passed, he became oblivious to the silent audience.

> —— *I have been one acquainted with the night.*
> *I have walked out in rain – and back in rain.*
> *I have outwalked the furthest city light . . .*

he was muttering to nobody in particular in the Zoffany Ward.

In Harry Chapman's heaven, Frank and Alice Chapman held each other's hands as lovers do. There was music by Bach and Schubert, and Fred Astaire led Queen Céleste in a perpetual waltz. Serene harmony prevailed.

But not, alas, for long. He awoke, in the dark, to sounds of weeping, whether from grief or pain he could not tell. He found the noise strangely consoling. It told him he was back in the real heavenly and hellish world.

Saturday Evening

SO HERE HE was again, where he had doubted he would ever be. He was at home among his books and pictures and music.

He had learned, from Dr Pereira, that the surgeon who had called him Sunshine was dead.

— An aneurism. Very swift.

The doctor warned that his own illness might recur. A benign tumour had been removed, but another could appear at any time.

— So my days are numbered, Doctor?

— Everyone's days are numbered, Harry. Even mine.

He had kissed Nancy, Marybeth and Veronica goodbye, and shaken hands with Maciek, Philip and his fruitseller saviour. Nancy had forbidden him to return, though she would miss his poems.

He sat in his favourite chair while Graham prepared supper. He hoped that he would come to agree with Jeremy Taylor that death is a harmless thing. A poor shepherd suffered it yesterday, as did a rich man. When Harry Chapman dies, he thought, a thousand others will die with him throughout the whole wide world.

The cat leapt on to his lap, curled herself into a multicoloured ball, and purred contentedly.

Harry Chapman offered Jack the ship-boy silent and heartfelt thanks for bringing the creaking vessel safely into port.

Friday

THOSE WORKING PARTS of Harry Chapman's body that could be beneficial to others – his heart, liver, kidneys and corneas – were removed at the hospital soon after his sudden death in the early hours of Sunday morning. Later that day, Graham informed the media of his friend's passing and started making arrangements for his funeral.

What was now left of the corporeal Harry Chapman was encased in a coffin of the plainest, cheapest wood. A clergyman would not be required to conduct the service, which was to be totally secular except for a reading of George Herbert's 'The Flower', with its invocation of a Lord of love who rescues the grief-stricken and benighted with His fulfilled promise of renewal and rejuvenation.

The mourners gathered at the chapel in Mortlake crematorium just before three o'clock on Friday afternoon. Graham greeted every one of them, accepting their condolences with the quiet dignity that was his by nature. He embraced and kissed Pamela Kenworth and the newly widowed Eleanor Duggan and shook hands with Wilf Granger, who remarked:

— It will be my turn next.

A stranger named Randolph Breeze introduced himself, along with his fiancée of twenty years, Miss Blanche Westermere.

— I had the exceptional good fortune of occupying the bed next to Mr Chapman in the Zoffany Ward. What a fascinating person. Miss Westermere and I have come to pay our last, alas, respects.

— How thoughtful of you.

— Mr Chapman's knowledge of T. S. Eliot was truly beyond pareil.

— Was it? He seldom talked about him. I know that he loathed Eliot's plays. He thought they were over encumbered with what he called 'well-bred dread'. But do excuse me, Mr – Wind, is it? –

— Breeze.

— Of course. My apologies. I must say hello to Dr Pereira and his team.

The doctor, Sister Nancy, Marybeth Myslawchuk and Maciek Nazwisko had managed to escape from their duties for an hour or so to say goodbye to Harry, the man with a thousand poems – they were sure it was at least a thousand – at his command. They didn't make a habit of going to patients' funerals, but this was an exception.

— I'm touched.

The ceremony was about to begin when a distraught elderly woman, whom many recognised as a famous novelist, burst into the chapel with several questions on her lips:

— Is this the right place? Is this the right time? Is this the right day? Have I come to the wrong funeral? It *is* Harry Chapman in the box, isn't it, and not somebody I've never heard of? Should I have gone to Putney instead? Harry *is* dead, isn't he? I'm not making it up, am I?

— No, Brenda, you're not making it up. Calm down. Yes, it's Harry in the box. Come and sit next to me.

— I'm sorry, Graham. I had a drinkie or two to settle my nerves and then I panicked. The taxi driver took me this way and that way, up hill and down dale, and all the time I was thinking I was on a fool's mission to nowhere. Oh, Harry, my poor lamb.

— Sit down, darling.

Eleanor Duggan opened the proceedings with the story of Paolo and Francesca, as recounted in Dante's *Inferno*. She read it in Italian and only translated the lines in which the poet has Francesca talking of the great sorrow that comes with remembered happiness. She was followed by the actor Jeremy Wilson, who read the final paragraph of Melville's 'Bartleby': 'Ah, Bartleby! Ah, humanity!'

Pamela went to the lectern, smiled at the congregation, and spoke from memory a poem by John Wilmot, Earl of Rochester, that Harry 'loved to distraction'.

> — *Ancient person, for whom I*
> *All the flattering youth defy,*
> *Long be it ere thou grow old,*
> *Aching, shaking, crazy, cold;*
> *But still continue as thou art,*
> *Ancient person of my heart.*
>
> *On thy withered lips and dry,*
> *Which like barren furrows lie,*
> *Brooding kisses I will pour*
> *Shall thy youthful heat restore,*
> *Nor from thee will ever part,*
> *Ancient person of my heart.*
>
> *The nobler part, which but to name*
> *In our sex would be counted shame,*
> *By age's frozen grasp possessed,*
> *From his ice shall be released,*

And soothed by my reviving hand,
In former warmth and vigour stand.
All a lover's wish can reach
For thy joy my love shall teach,
And for thy pleasure shall improve
All that art can add to love.
Yet still I love thee without art,
Ancient person of my heart.

And then Graham read 'The Flower', as Harry had instructed, in a steady voice. In the closing seven minutes, there was a recorded performance of Webern's orchestration of the fugue (*ricercata*) from Bach's *The Musical Offering*, which Harry had requested to be played in honour of the Duchess of Bombay.

There was a champagne reception, or wake, at the house in Hammersmith. The buffet had been prepared by a chef from Rome and Graham hoped that the guests would stay sober enough to appreciate Massimiliano's subtle cooking. Brenda, who was indifferent to everything other than fried eggs and bacon, had already attained the very peak, the Everest, of drunkenness in a remarkably short time and had concealed herself beneath Harry's desk, with her sleeping head stuck in his waste-paper basket.

There were two uninvited guests, two notable gatecrashers, in the forms of Mr Breeze and his ageing bride-to-be Blanche Westermere. They arrived with Wilf Granger, who assured Graham that they were an enchanting couple. They had listened to his tales of woe – dodgy prostate; dicky ticker; diabetes and an ingrowing toenail, not to say his inability to get Dick Turpin to stand and deliver – with the utmost, and he really meant the utmost, sympathy.

This was the farewell party Harry would have wanted, Graham thought as midnight approached. There had been some serious conversations, but the farcical spirit had finally prevailed. Brenda had left wearing the waste-paper basket like an Easter bonnet, and that was a vision Harry would have cherished. Then Wilf revealed that he had written a cheque for a thousand pounds to the delightful Mr Breeze in order to be the proud owner of T. S. Eliot's false teeth.

— If my own fall out, as they look like doing, I can always wear his.

When he was alone at last, Graham noticed that there was a letter addressed to him on the doormat. There was no stamp on it. He read:

Dear Mr Weaver,
    Please forgive me intruding on your grief. Your partner Harry was very kind to my late unhappy brother Ralph and I bless him for his kindness. May he rest in peace. I will toast his lovely memory with a glass of sherry.
    Yours,
    Beryl

Graham dimmed the lights and sat in Harry's armchair and welcomed the purring cat into his arms.

Mary, Sam and Roy Adams; Thomas Bailey; Arthur and Helen Maud Bailey; Joan Bailey; David and Ellen Bailey; Gabriel Bailey; Beryl Bainbridge; Vanni, Noris and Piero Bartolozzi; Carl Bonn; Mabel Burgess; Angela Carter; Kathleen Church; Elizabeth David; Noel Davis; Frank Day; Tom and Peggy d'Errico; Alice and Hal Dickey; Rose Donnelly; Sadie Dunnett; Sandor Eles; Michael Elliott; Ilona Ference; Gordon Gostelow; Jane and Geoffrey Grigson; Paolo Guasconi; David Healy; Connie Highton; Reverend Stephan Hopkinson; John and Sylvia Hove; Russell Hunter; Leslie Hurry; Harald Jensen; Terence Kilmartin; Richard Lord; Colin Mackenzie; Ken McGregor; Robert Medley; Patrick O'Connor; Vincent Osborne; Muriel Philipson; William Plomer; Betty and J. F. Powers; Oliver Reynolds; Ian Richardson; John D. Roberts; Bryan Robertson; Alan Ross; Jeremy Round; Bernice Rubens; Lorna Sage; John Schlesinger; John Stocken; Elizabeth Taylor; Stephen Tumim; Dorothea Wallace; John T. Wharton; Angus Wilson; Casper Wrede.

A NOTE ON THE TYPE

Linotype Garamond Three – based on seventeenth-century copies of Claude Garamond's types, cut by Jean Jannon. This version was designed for American Type Founders in 1917, by Morris Fuller Benton and Thomas Maitland Cleland and adapted for mechanical composition by Linotype in 1936.